Tales from the Canyons of the Damned

PRESENTED BY USA TODAY BESTSELLING AUTHOR
DANIEL ARTHUR SMITH

Tales from the Canyons of the Damned 41

First Edition

Special thanks to editor Artie Cabrera

ISBN: 978-1-946-777-89-8

Cover By Daniel Arthur Smith

Horror Fiction from Holt Smith ltd
Agroland
Tower
Attack of the Kung Fu Mummies

For Susan, Tristan, & Oliver, as all things are.

The Slow Apocalypse

Liviu Surugiu
Translation By
Sebi Simion and Daniel Arthur Smith

Elise vanished while I was speaking to her on the phone. She was saying something about the place where we would have dinner. I don't remember where it was. I do remember, however, the way her voice quaked when she described her mother *blackening*. That I understood later to be terror and disbelief. Then she screamed, and the call dropped.

Immediately, I tapped her name on my screen to call her back but my phone would not connect, there was no signal. There was nothing.

People have always imagined an end where everybody dies at once, the way we imagine the dinosaurs vaporizing after the meteor. A great single extinction-causing event. It's in books, the movies, religion, especially religion. No one has ever been content with the idea of dying alone.

That's the main thing about the end of the world, apocalypse, it's a clean sweep, we don't die one at a time. It's just so much easier to comprehend, I suppose. Nobody imagines a slow apocalypse, which ironically is how the majority of the dinosaurs did vanish from the Earth.

It began in Salem. Salem, New Jersey, to be clear. That's where I witnessed it. It was afternoon. A solid black line appeared across the length of the horizon to the west, a long stripe, not tall enough to completely cover the buildings. In fact, for a while, the serrated profile of the Wilmington skyline could still be seen far away, past the Delaware River. Until the buildings on the horizon sunk into it one by one. That's when we realized it was moving, coming from the west the way one expects night to come from the east, engulfing the building and land beneath them as it traveled the Earth's curve.

The long black band travelled over the fields, hills, and mountains, swallowing them with the same indifference it took the highways, cities, parks, cars—or people.

Since only the ground and what was on that was disappearing, the late afternoon sun could still be seen hovering above, beyond the ominous black ribbon, a sun that should have later been setting.

The way the blackness appeared, the way it traveled from the west, it seemed the world was no longer obeying any laws of physics.

Elise had been my girlfriend since shortly after I had come to the States to continue my studies, almost two years.

After our conversation was cut off with her scream, I immediately stormed from class to the parking lot, then frantically drove as quickly as I could to her neighborhood, rolling through stop signs, through changing lights, repeatedly tapping her name to reach her on my phone, the whole time cussing the lack of service. I didn't know that the apocalypse had already begun.

Just before reaching Elise's block, the cars ahead all slowed, then abruptly stopped, their brake lights flaring all at once, and with a screech of my tires, I slammed my brakes, too. My heart was pounding. Behind me, I could hear people swearing and honking, the skidding of tires, and what must have been a domino cascade of cars crashing into one another, bumper to bumper. But those of us in front of the stalled traffic were indifferent to the mayhem behind. We stepped out of our cars dumbfounded, gaping at the eerie black wave in awe.

Up close, it was a tall wall of sheer darkness, a void I'd guess fifty-feet high, slowly moving towards us, enveloping the rooftops of the tallest buildings as it crept forward. The upper floors of the few high rises appeared to levitate, while below them there was nothing. Then slowly they sunk, collapsing downward, allowing the black to claim the balconies, attics, skylights, and chimneys. People ran across the flat roofs as they would from a fire or tsunami and launched themselves from the ledges, but they fell into the wave and never reached the ground.

Kevin, Elise's neighbor, was strolling down the alley, a block beyond where I stood, headphones on, not knowing what was going on behind him. I yelled to him, "Kevin! Kevin! Look behind you! Run!" But with the headphones on he couldn't hear me. His dog, trailing on a leash behind him stopped, spun to face the incoming wall of darkness, then started barking. Then the poor animal disappeared. Kevin didn't realize it, because the leash had been severed by invisible fangs and dangled empty behind him. He looked up in time to see me waving my arms. His face shifted from a smile to puzzlement and he stopped walking to process the commotion. Then he too was gone.

Blocked with cars, the street where I stood had become a parking lot. Shouts and honking persisted back where one couldn't see the creeping black curtain, still hidden by the walls it was about to consume. We in the front said nothing to warn them. We just stared at the long ribbon of black as it slowly absorbed the street a block over and then the buildings closer to us. The asphalt disappeared along with the trees. Lawns, houses, office buildings, and parked cars, everything was being wiped out by the infinite eraser of an anti-creator.

Some of the people around me were muttering explanations of what we were witnessing, but their voices seemed far from me, and I can't remember what exactly they said, but there were words like—antimatter, black hole, wormhole, parallel universe, Allah, God. It could've been anything, really. I know only that my heart was pulling me towards Elise, the image of her in trouble, reaching out for me, filled my head so that my only focus was on her, and that focus was telling me to stay put, in case she had somehow ran through the buildings ahead of Kevin, somehow would run out the door of the building closest to me. I even drew my eyes from the blackness of the door, expecting my vision to play out, expecting to see the door fling open, and Elis bursting through. Then something clicked in my mind, and I understood at the moment was that we were witnessing the end, Elise wasn't running out, and I realized that I couldn't stand still because that black wall of darkness moving toward me wasn't going to stop. It was moving at a slow, but at a constant pace. I had to flee, but I couldn't.

Though my mind was telling me to run. I couldn't. My feet were still frozen, while others around, braver than myself, approached the black and poked sticks, umbrellas, and suitcases at the strange and uniform wave. They backed slowly away to curiously examine the severed objects they had half emerged into the veil, and then the bravest amongst them stopped to see how it felt to go from full daylight to darkness.

I was terrified. My stomach cramped, my heart raced, and my mouth went dry.

The first man to test the dark had his back to us and had frozen in place facing the black wall. He stood tall and firm as if at attention as the night covered him, enveloped him, like the water of a black lake. I couldn't know what he saw at that moment, if his eyes were registering or if the electric impulse sent from his pupils brought back any images to his brain at all.

Another man turned his back to the unknown, smiled at us watching him, then closed his eyes. His mind was engulfed, while his face was still smiling at us, then he rapidly vanished as the blackness persisted forward, immersing his temples, cheeks, and eyes, all the way to his lips, chin, and the tip of his nose.

After watching the first two, a young woman took her turn. As the first man faced the wall and the second faced us, she seemed to decide to embrace the oncoming black wall sideways, with her left side facing the wave, her right side facing us. I could clearly see half of her face from where I was standing, while she was seeing something else with the other half. And as the night swallowed the left side of her face, I swear I saw a tear emerge from her right eye. Then the blackness swallowed her face whole. When all that was left of her was her right hand, her fingers twitched—and then the spell was broken. Screams

5

erupted around me, and from me maybe, I think I heard my screams amongst them, I'm not sure. But then, almost against my will, carried by the human flood, I started running away from Elise's place. The eastward moving mass split and separated into several smaller crowds, like prehistoric people running from a mammoth which had escaped from a trap set by them.

It was coming for us at that slow constant pace, so we could look at its featureless face now and then, and I remember doing just that, stopping and looking back, as did others. We realized that we could run faster than the *end of the world*. But to our horror, we saw crippled people in wheelchairs, left behind, swallowed, atom by atom, and there was nothing to be done, no going back. No going back for the dogs left howling in abandoned apartments, the cats mesmerized by the moving darkness. All we could do was go forward, but for how long? How far away could we retreat? How much more would it advance?

A woman that had run ahead of me and stopped to look back, gestured to me. Barely breathing she asked, "Did you see?" She gasped for air then pointing upward beyond me and added, "The wires on the poles!"

I spun to look but could offer no explanation. The cables remained extended into the black, even though the poles were gone. It was the same with other things that should have collapsed, heavier things, houses, and overpasses, continued to stand on our side, even if important parts of their structures were gone first, then vanished without a sound.

The incoming wave of darkness gave me chills, a physical quiver that ran up the center of my spine and squeezed my neck in its clawed grip. More than once I bent forward with nausea, but there was nothing to release. The blackness brought dread, brought horror, it was like someone had opened an infinite door over the Earth and let in another world's night.

The sinister wall advanced as mute as death, stifling every noise, from planks to the walls crashing down, while other parts of them were still falling.

I decided that in fact, it was death itself. It had always been her, only we had never truly seen her before to recognize her when she came. There's only a brief slice of a moment between life and death, and that moment was finally visible.

I continued to flee from it. I ran down side streets, through alleys, over fences and through yards, I must've run the best part of a mile when I realized I had separated from those running beside me and found myself on street where, though slow, traffic was still moving. Hands to my hips, I took in huge breaths, my blood rushing with the new oxygen I took in. I noticed a taxi approaching, hailed it, and when he pulled to the curb, I hopped in.

Catching my breath, I said to the driver, "Please. Get me out of the city."

"What address?" the man asked, not sensing my anxiety.

He was fidgeting with the radio, trying to get it to work. It wouldn't because the antenna in Salem was already gone. But I said nothing, not a word about the chaos I had left behind, maybe because of shock, maybe for fear of not being able to save myself.

"Go east," I said, my lungs still aching for breath. "Take me east!"

The driver, a heavy old scruff faced man who smelled of the heat of the day, gave me a stern glance in his rearview mirror, but then pulled the lever down on the meter and without hesitation for oncoming traffic drove across the four lanes to take the first right on a road going east.

Throughout the trip, not a word was spoken.

My breathing soothed, my heart beat slowed, my mind drifted.

Half an hour later the driver pulled the taxi to the curb next to a huge painted sign that read *Welcome to Millville*. He stopped the meter and said, "That's as far as I go."

I looked at the back of his head as if I was just waking up from a dream. My mind had become numb on the drive over, my thoughts, if any, a mess. I was dazed and confused, my thinking a jumble. As reason retook me, the first images were crazed. Had I dreamed without falling asleep? Maybe it had all just been a dream. Then I remembered—east. I leaned forward to try to get the driver to see my face, but then met his eyes in the mirror. "Can you go a bit further?" I asked. "Please... I'll pay."

"No, sorry," he said. "This is the edge of my zone and I have to get back..." Seeing no change on my face he continued, "I have to. I'm off in an hour. It would be better if you just get another cab or maybe, maybe take the train."

"Okay," I said, passively agreeing. It made sense. I reached into my pocket and pulled out a few folded bills, more than enough to cover the fare, then handed them to him.

The driver didn't bother counting the money. "Have a good day," he said. Then added, "I'm going back to the depot..." as if to convince me to leave.

"Right," I said. I opened the door, and as I stepped out onto the curb, I looked up at the sky. Huge flocks of birds were passing high above, underneath the clouds, barely audible, their color the gray of places far away.

They were heading due east. To the ocean. Only the ocean was that way.

A panic shot through me. "Don't go!" I shouted to the driver. I grabbed the car door I'd just shut, but it was already locked. "Don't go back... stay!"

But he didn't stay, rather he gunned the gas rocking the whole taxi as he sped from the curb into a u-turn, looking at me as he passed back by as if I were a madman, and I didn't have time to say anything else.

Apart from being in Millville, I didn't know exactly where I was or even what street I was on. There was silence all around me. The block was empty. Apart from the fleeing taxi, the street was empty, both ways—no one else was coming from the west. I considered that for a moment, that no one else was fleeing toward me, the only obvious answer being that Millville wasn't really to the east, but to the south-east of Salem, rather diagonally to the direction the madness was going.

Pondering the absence of others, I turned and walked toward the city center.

I somewhat knew little about Millville. I had visited it with Elise a couple of times. The image of my girlfriend sent another quiver up my spine and sent my hair standing straight from the sensation. Had she died? What was going on behind that darkness, the veil in which even light couldn't escape? And all of those behind it, had they all disintegrated, or gone to a different world, a different time? Was there any other world, after all? A world beyond ours? Was there a God?

The rush of thoughts made me dizzy. I took in a breath, and then another slower one, and then another, to focus, to get my bearings.

Breathing slow, I calmed my mind and started to slowly sort things out. I was on the city's west side. I knew that much.

In all my time in America I had never before seen so few cars on the street. Even the parking lots were empty. That was noted. I decided it meant that the people here had already found out about the blackness and had left. I wasn't supposed to stay much longer either. The houses around me seemed abandoned, blinds down, no one around. I could only hear a faint screeching noise, most likely an unoiled swing moved by the wind, in an abandoned playground. I strained my eyes toward what I thought to be school, in search of the source.

Something touched my shoulder.

I jumped forward, twirling away from whatever it was, my stomach falling deep into my gut.

The something had been the hand of a young black police officer.

"It's okay, calm down," he said, a kind calm on his face. "You're not from around here, are you?"

"I, uh…I come from Salem!" I said, sighing with relief. "I just got here in a cab." I raised my hand to gesture toward the direction I had come.

The young officer grinned. "I thought you came from France!" he said. "Your accent…"

I didn't correct him. Rather, overwhelmed with the adrenalin, hormones, and emotion, I wanted to hug him.

He glanced down at his watch. "Took you just over thirty minutes to get here," he said, as if he had been waiting for me and I was late.

"Um. Yeah. Something like that, I think…"

"Hm," he nodded.

"How did you know?" I asked.

"That's when it hit Salem." He gestured his chin east. "Salem runaways went *straight* for the ocean. Nobody's here except for you."

It was as I deduced.

"You have some time though," he added.

"Sorry?" I asked confused.

"You're twenty miles east of it," he explained. "You've earned yourself fifteen hours."

He must have sensed I was puzzled because he added, "Because the *Madness* is advancing by one-point-eighty-six miles per hour. Unless that changes, it's going to be here tomorrow morning. Fifteen hours."

"The Madness," I said nodding. It was the first time I learned the name of the phenomena and the speed at which it traveled. It was as if the mystery had been partially solved. I started to speak, "Do you—" but in the excitement I choked up a bit and my throat had seized tight.

"Take your time," he said.

I nodded then started again. "Do you know what it is?" I asked.

"No one does. Some say it's some kind of joke, a trick, like David Copperfield. Only David Copperfield isn't going through a wall, the wall is going through us."

"You think so?" I said, clinging hopefully to his words. "I mean, it's a poor joke, but if it is some sort of trick, that would mean no one has died."

"Yeah. Well. Others," he went on, "say it's an out of control experiment. Anyway, almost everyone's left Millville. People around here are used to hurricanes, they know how to move fast if they have to evacuate. We should be gone by nightfall, too."

"Gone to where? Where to?"

"East. Same as everybody else."

"But we're so close to the ocean," I said. "There's nowhere to run."

"From here it's thirty-seven miles to Atlantic City. That's another twenty hours onto the fifteen to get here. This apocalypse is slow only to those who are far from it. For us, it's coming really damn fast."

He was right. I already felt like I couldn't breathe. My heart was pounding even though I stood in place, as if it wanted to get away from me.

"Twenty more hours onto the fifteen to get here," I repeated. "What then? What if it won't stop?"

The man looked around, and even if there was no one there, he said in a low voice:

"You know, it's a weapon. Made by the Chinese, obviously. The Russians wouldn't do this. It's designed so you can't go around it, and it's sweeping all of us towards the Atlantic. It's basically making us get on planes and ships, taking us directly to them, making us surrender, so we can do cheap labor for them—maybe even for free."

An old woman appeared from the side of the house beside us, her slippers dragging through the withered leaves in the yard. Perhaps she had been studying me from behind the blinds and decided to come out after she had seen the young policeman.

"Hey, Billy!" she yelled, though only a few feet away. "What's going on?"

"Nothing, Professor Jablonski!" he replied. "Absolutely nothing! Radio's only working on the army's frequency now and the Internet's been down a good fifteen minutes!"

"Do you know what this is about?" I asked the woman.

As she approached, I realized that she was even older than she first appeared. A web of wrinkles spread across her crepe-paper-thin spotted cheeks, and her fine hair was dyed the youthful red that only comes from a bottle. She shrugged:

She stopped yelling, but obviously hard of hearing continued to speak louder than needed. "The last time I watched the news," she said. "They were saying it looked like a meridian. That it's coming in a straight line, from one pole to the other." She drew a line alongside an invisible sphere. "So they've named it the Black Meridian. It's going one-point-eighty-six miles per hour. So, it will need about a year and a half to cross the whole world."

Billy the officer nodded when she mentioned the speed, as if having this one bit of knowledge gave them some kind of control.

She paused for a bit and went on:

"It looks like a giant Moebius ring to me, allowing continuous passage between two areas usually separated."

I kept my composure, pretending to understand what that meant, then asked, hopeful, "Do you think that those consumed by it... are gone?"

She met my eyes and paused before answering. It was obvious that the question was challenging. Maybe she felt like she was in class again, facing her students and a difficult problem. Maybe she thought she had left someone behind. Or maybe I hadn't spoken loud enough. I was about to repeat the question she finally said, "No. And just so you can see, I'm confident in my theories, and I'm not leaving. I didn't leave when the last hurricane came, I'm not leaving now. If the Earth were to be truly swallowed, piece by piece, like an orange, it should affect gravity, atmosphere—"

The young man interrupted her. "I'll swing by tonight to leave the fine in your mailbox, Professor. You know I have to; the evacuation order is clear. Everyone should leave Millville today."

"I'll pay it," she replied. "Just like I paid the one last year. I wasn't frightened by a hurricane. I won't be frightened by..." She gazed off to the west. "By whatever this is."

"Professor Jablonski," I said, hanging on to her words. "What do you think happened to those who stayed? Those in Salem?"

"Nothing," she said flatly. "What can happen when you're hit by nothing? ...Nothing! That's what. Maybe they don't even know it. How do we know a wave of nothing isn't passing by as we speak?"

I thought of Elise again. My God, was she still alive?

"Shame," the old professor added, walking away. "I taught in vain, all my life. The laws of physics no longer apply—that's the real anarchy!"

I watched her disappear back around the side of her house. Then I realized that the young officer was also walking away. I was standing there on the sidewalk alone, and the fear of the unknown, the dread, was embracing me in its tight grip once more, as if I was facing the greatest evil seen by man.

I started down the sidewalk, walking, then jogging, then checking through the windows of the remaining cars. I found luck in a blue Toyota rav4. The fob key was in the console, carelessly forgotten by its owner. I hopped in, pushed the button ignition, and the car started. Without hesitation I shifted the car into gear and drove off.

I thought about what the officer had said, and if he was right, I had to find a radio that could tune in to the army's frequency, whatever that was. It was the only way

I could find what was happening in the world and what to do next.

Almost out of instinct, I headed for the interstate and started going north, where my subconscious was telling me I would find more than a radio. Four months before, Elise and I had passed an abandoned military base. Elise...

The base had been long abandoned but given that everything on the road from Millville was also deserted, it didn't seem out of place.

I passed through the open chain link gate and followed the signs to the PX, expecting to find a warehouse. Instead, I came upon a large shopping center with a huge red and blue X above the glass doors next to the word *EXCHANGE* in five-foot-high letters. That place, caressed by the setting sun, would soon be covered in darkness—forever. Though abandoned, the military store looked like it could come back to life at any time, the parking lot however was full of undisturbed weeds, sprouting from the web of cracks across its surface. I pulled the Toyota between two of the of white lines gridded out to designate proper parking spots, turned off the engine, and headed toward the doors.

That was my last mistake.

About ten feet from the double glass doors there was a loud deafening crack and my leg buckled from an intense, sharp sting to the side. I attempted to straighten it but the pain overwhelmed me and I fell toward the concrete, blacking out before I landed.

When I came to, I found myself sitting on the floor, my back to the cement block wall, my hands cuffed to a rusted radiator on one side of me and a steel door with a long slit of a window running its length next to the stainless handle. Whoever had chained me up must have also tended my wound and stopped the bleeding. I had never been shot before, but the pain had dulled to an ache, and looking at my thigh through my torn pants it didn't seem that bad. What was really bad was that I was chained up, while a mysterious wave of some-dark-thing was drawing closer. What's more, I wasn't even sure how much time had passed.

"You've been lying there all night," a voice croaked. "I must have botched the painkiller dose."

I barely managed to turn my head around. I didn't see the man who spoke, but by the three large garage doors on the far wall, I figured I was in the PX loading bay. The corners were dark, but was a large, eerie room, empty except for a few random pallets scattered across the concrete floor and covered in dust. The large, dirty windows that spanned the length of the wall high above the garage doors were lit white with sunlight, but the light didn't cast down to the grey shadowy floor. It looked like the coop of some long-dead pigeons.

"Why did you shoot me?" I asked. "Who are you?"

I was scared. As I turned my head back, I caught my reflection in a shard of glass on the floor and jumped. Yesterday before school I had looked twenty five. Right then in that little piece of glass I looked as if I had been in a coma since then. My wavy dark hair was mussed and white from the dust I had been dragged through, while my face looked pink and wrinkly from the floor I had been laying my head on.

"Colonel Sternfels! In..." and the croaky voice stopped.

This time I honed in on him, a tall figure in the corner shadows. I squinted to focus and though the features of his face were hard to make out I determined that the man was old, at least sixty, wearing a uniform approximately the same age.

Oddly enough, I was not afraid, maybe because I feared the incoming wall of black more than I did that simple man. At least I was able to see him. Compared to the unknown that was devouring the whole world, I felt like I had known the so-called colonel for hundreds of thousands of years, since man first walked the Earth.

Antagonized by his silence, I finished his sentence. "In retirement," I said.

That provoked him. The old man stormed from the shadows shouting. "A true army man is never in retirement! There has to be a new word for that! Do you hear me! A new word!"

I breathed in. Great. He was crazy.

"Colonel Sternfels," I said. "Until someone comes up with another word, will you please undo these cuffs? In case you don't know, there's something out there, something dangerous, and it's getting really close…"

"That's why I caught you," he said in a tone justifying his actions.

I awkwardly shuffled my body all the way around so I could see him better.

Up close, Sternfels looked a lot older than he did in the shadows, at least seventy-five. His unshaven cheeks were yellowed with the jaundice of a failing liver and covered in field of brilliant white bristles, his blue eyes, faded by the light that had gone through them, were sunken and bloodshot. He had been in retirement a long time and the thought of being able to take him down gave me hope, prompting me to act weaker than I actually was.

"That's Hell that's coming for us," he went on. "It came up from under the ground and it's coming to sweep us away. Forgive me, young man, but ah…" His right eye twitched as he drifted off.

Yeah, definitely crazy, and the fact that he was insane brought me no joy. Especially since a lingering pain was growing in my leg.

"Painkillers wearing off?" he said, watching me closely.

I was struggling to control myself.

"No, I've just gone a bit numb!" I lied, afraid of being sedated again.

Sternfels walked over to the far side of the radiator and dragged a large flat panel TV from the wall around to face me and sat down on the floor beside me in front of the door, but not close enough for me touch him in any way except for maybe my legs. I tried moving them, but the pain in my thigh was too intense.

"Watch this," he said, leaning forward and to plug a memory stick into the side. "It's the last news broadcast the Americans ever saw on TV!"

He held a remote for the flat panel in his hand. He brought it close to his face then tapped a button and looked back at the screen. The screen lit up blue, the digital designation AV1 in the upper right corner. Happy with the this, Sternfels' tongue leaked out over his lip as he let his finger drop onto the remote one more time. A moving image filled the screen.

For a couple of minutes, I forgot about the pain and the predicament I was in. The image of the thing that was invading the world was more shocking than my current condition, and simply watching it move and devour was hypnotizing. It took a minute or two before I realized that the footage was on a loop, but that did lessen the mystique. It was filmed from a helicopter. Fighter jets like the ones from Top Gun, passed high over the black wall at great speed. Missiles launched from their bellies toward the slow avalanche, but even at its shallow height, there were no explosions, beneath the surface or rising above it.

Sternfels noted the same poignant fact. "Hellfires," he said. "If they do actually explode..." he drifted off then winced again. "Maybe there's already nothing left. Maybe something is happening with the time, and it's wound forward or back one second, so nothing is hitting its target, or maybe it's hitting its target and the explosion will occur in our time an hour, a day, or a week from now." He shook his head. "Who knows which corner of the universe it's getting lost in, out by Jupiter, the other side of the galaxy. Just like the people caught in this..." A drift, a wince.

"I thought you said it was Hell," I said.

"But does anyone know what Hell really is?" he replied. "The vacuum of space could be Hell. The middle of a mountain. They've launched hundreds of bombs, lasers, and dropped stuff from satellites... No reaction!"

He pointed the remote at the panel and turned up the volume. Until then I had thought it was just the video. I was seeing the same footage for the fourth time.

"The radar, sonar, UV, and radiation detectors, everything that we have pointed at... this thing... are getting no replies!" the reporter in the helicopter was desperately shouting. "All the probes and drones we've launched... track-laying robots... it's only doing one thing: it keeps advancing and gives nothing back!"

"I wonder what's happening underground," Sternfels was muttering. "No imagination, these fools! If only they'd dig some tunnels or if some elite units would hide in some salt mine...? Or under the sea! Although I've heard on the radio that the wave is advancing the same in the Arctic Ocean and not even a fish can get away from it. Before the signal died, they said that a nuclear submarine wasn't able to retreat due to a technical error and its whole compliment and cargo was swallowed piece by piece…"

"Do you have a radio? Is there one around?" I repeated. "That's what I came here for, so I could find out what to do, where to go, so I can escape…"

Sternfels looked at me with something resembling pity.

"It's not working anymore," he said.

Powerless, I slumped down next to the radiator. The images on the flat panel had overwhelmed me.

"Look at that flock of birds!" I said, startled. "They must be pigeons…"

"Starlings," the colonel corrected. "I saw them too. The reporter didn't say anything, he was too focused on the bombs they were dropping."

The flock was flying increasingly lower, their murmations, a giant amoeba dilating and contracting under the lens of a microscope, until it started touching the black surface and disappeared in its blind mirror one bird at a time.

Talking to that old man, I had forgotten for a moment that he was the madman and I, the prisoner. Maybe it was rest of the world and me who were disturbed and not him. What values were still in place? What was right and wrong?

And then the next thought, my God, where would I run, even if I could escape? With my leg wound I wouldn't even get to be one step ahead of the Slow End of the World!

"Who's Elise?" he asked all of a sudden.

"Sorry?"

"You were talking about her in your sleep. You were raving, actually. Must have been those pills, I can't really remember what I gave you."

That was unsettling.

"Elise is… was… my girlfriend."

"She was left *behind*?"

"Yes." Left *behind*, I thought. A quaint misnomer. I didn't leave her anywhere, if anything, she was taken.

"What about your parents? Are you French?"

"Dead for a long time," I said. "I have a rich uncle in Paris. He sent me here for my studies."

In that instant, the cuffs on my wrists began to vibrate. It was subtle at first, traveling through the pipes of the radiator, but then I felt it through the floor. A subtle vibration, increasing in intensity by the second, building to a full rumble. Dust started coming out of the ceiling. As if the world was a huge fake and someone was tearing down the décor.

"The army!" the colonel shouted, getting to his feet. "We're in the middle of a war!" he spun to peek out the window in the door.

I strained to turn myself from the radiator to peer through a narrow slit, where I discovered that he was right. First, barreling through the gates from the west, one after the other, came the convoy of military trucks filled with soldiers and cannons. Then the ground started shaking even more and a column of tanks appeared, tearing over the chain link perimeter fences side-by-side. I had never seen real-life tanks before. One of them stopped right in front of the door, merely fifteen, twenty feet from us. It spun, turned its turret, and fired backwards.

"My God, what time is it?" I yelled. "How much time do we have?"

"Ten am!" Sternfels replied just as loudly. "We're very close! Are you ready? Hell should be here any minute!!"

And it came.

I saw nothing but blackness. Terrified, I tugged the chain that bound my hands to the radiator.

The darkness was coming from the west, inevitably devouring everything in its wake. Getting closer every second. Through the window, past the array of fleeing humvees, tanks, and personnel carriers, I could see tree branches swaying and then swallowed whole, abandoned towers glinting in the sun one last time, the concrete floor caressed by the shadow of an eclipse where both the sun and the universe were meeting their end.

A tank stuck in place was still firing, and with the last dregs of reason I was wondering why they were launching projectiles on places they had just passed through. What if there were still people there? What if they were somehow alive? ...The track came to life spinning in place while its other end, covered in darkness, couldn't move. Then the turret opened, and two soldiers jumped out, before the tank was fully engulfed.

People and animals were running across the concrete while the *Madness*, as Billy the cop had called it, advanced slowly, calm, like a whale picking plankton. Some of them were falling, others were too tired and had resorted to crawling. Those about to meet their fate stood in place, waiting for the unyielding wall.

Sternfels had left my side and strolled to the center of the loading bay.

"Let me go," I begged. "For Christ's sake, let me go, man!"

But the Colonel had other plans. He spun to face me, a smile as crazy as his mind, across his yellow face. "In the name of the Devil!" he yelled. "Thou shalt stay here!"

Then Sternfels broke into some sort of chant. "I will offer you myself! For…"

The far wall beyond him, with its three garage doors and line of dirty windows near the ceiling was going away slowly, noiseless, then death entered the loading bay. The black curtain was with us. It was crawling towards us, deceiving, mute, inexorable, at a speed barely under a meter per second. Seen up close, in a closed space, it didn't look that slow anymore. My God, it was seven seconds away from me!

Sternfels saw it too late, not realizing it had come in, and I said nothing as I watched him fall backwards, to the floor that had suddenly started shifting like that of a sinking ship. I could barely hear him muttering as his face was disappearing into the tar-colored oblivion.

Death was a breath away. I could see its perfectly smooth, black surface, where no other colors dwelled. It was coming for me in my final moments of life.

Then, it came to me. With a wail and a howl thrust my legs up and around and I swung around the radiator. As the wall moved close, I pulled the cuffs taut, and as the chain of the cuffs slipped into the black, I flew backwards, the chain cut off by the black. Beyond the radiator was a window, with my wounded leg on fire, I dove through into the glass headfirst using the strength of my skull to shatter the glass. The shards fells silently then disappeared, sucked up into the black air behind me. I rolled in a somersault and didn't even feel the impact of my landing because my legs were in so much pain. I was outside, on the pavement.

Huge pain tore through rest of my body when I stood, stemming from my wounded leg. I was in tears, but the infinite wall was rising high above me, making everything dark… I was one step away from the void!

Fighting pain with adrenalin I willed myself forward, I hobbled, I fell, I crawled, I got up again. Slowly building distance between myself and the black.

Out of the base and into the town, limping through abandoned cars. Screaming, begging, cursing, and crying.

I stopped for a moment to catch my breath and I heard a shot nearby. A man came out from behind a restaurant, wiping his bloody hand on his shirt, while pushing a bike with the other. He looked at me for a split second, got on the bike and rode to the end of the street.

In broad daylight, the darkness was still coming.

The drugstore's windows were broken when I reached it, panting, as death slowly crept toward me.

Sweat streamed down my forehead, my hair was soaked, and my whole body shook with fever and fear. I fumbled through drawers, one eye out the storefront, watching the street get dark. Painkillers, energy supplements—I swallowed them all at once in a handful then started again, dragging my wounded leg behind me, barely keeping my distance from the terrifying blackness.

The army that had sped by was nowhere to be seen nor was anyone else around on the garbage-littered streets of dented cars and lost luggage. It's funny how many things people can leave behind them when they're running away from death. It looked as if a tsunami had got to them and then gone back with the tide, stealing their possessions. Anything that was too heavy, holding them back. Backpacks, lunchboxes, clothes, flashlights, laptops, and even phones were the remnants of a civilization—remnants which I was trying to make my way through. Was I really the only survivor, alone in facing the unknown?

That's when I heard the helicopter.

And then I saw it.

At first, I wanted to get to the middle of the street so I could shout or wave, but something held me back. It wasn't coming from the east. It was coming from the other side, above the slow, black avalanche of death. It wasn't a rescue mission, it wasn't looking for survivors. On the contrary, the pilot only seemed interested in the otherworldly wave.

The helicopter touched down gingerly on the road. Across the side was the word Jovski. I didn't know what that meant. The door opened and two men in flashy-looking, well-tailored black suits jumped out. They looked at the street for a split second, not seeing me cowering behind a dumpster.

Four more men in flight suits and helmets jumped out of the helicopter right after, floating like gods a few feet above the ground on hover boards. I'd seen the boards before, they were the expensive Zapata fly-boards. They wouldn't fly long, but they could easily soar over the edge of the black wave. The two suited men leapt back into the helicopter, and then it lifted back into the air. The four didn't hesitate, they were in perfect balance on their boards, and once clear of the chopper, they did the most insane thing I could picture.

I would later find out that the new sport had its own name, death-surf. Instead of waves, the challenge was the black mane of the unknown. They were millionaires looking for fun. The world's richest had come to say goodbye to it in their own way. Like the four horsemen of the apocalypse, they rode on the back of darkness, whooping and hollering.

I realized in my hideout that in the span of only a day and a night, I had turned into a rat-man, fearful, cautious, and not trusting even of my fellow men.

I should have just kept moving east, but I couldn't believe my eyes. On their fly-boards, the death surfers were quickly navigating through the buildings surrounded by the edge of a parallel universe. When they got too close to the black wave, the blue gas of the jet turbines was deviated, absorbed by the walking void, making their flotation even more difficult, as if a second, unseen tide was racing against them.

It was insane.

Conscious of the ever creeping death, I too kept moving, from behind the dumpster to an overturned RV, then to a building which also disappeared after a few minutes. The helicopter rose and dipped couple of times, while the death-surfers were flying over the slow torrent of blackness.

I was still hesitating, trying to decide whether I should get close to the helicopter or not. I was under the weird impression that they were all bad guys—when one of the surfers crashed right in front of me. He had flown too close to the edge of death, sheared off the bottom of his fly-board, and the gas within it was swallowed by the black before it could burn. He was up a good thirty feet when he flew from the board down onto the pavement. The board, closer to the wave quickly vanished into the nothingness. He would have been consumed too, but luckily for him, I was a few feet away and sprung to his aid. I grabbed him by his shoulders and dragged him away as fast as I could, but he remained limp, and I suspected at once that he hadn't been too lucky. The helmet had protected his face when he slammed to the pavement. However, when I removed it, I saw that his neck had been broken. He was about my age, and he was dead. We could hear the boards of the others, but they were beyond my line of sight, the surfers were just going around the other side of a building that was being covered.

I took the dead man's clothes. The wave was a few seconds away by the time I finished changing. I slipped on the shoes and helmet while I limped over toward the helicopter waiting around on the next block.

With adrenaline coursing through their veins, the other three surfers flew shouting above me, and I got into the helicopter just after they did.

We all buckled our seatbelts while we rose above the black lava.

The man across from me reached for an audio plug and stuck it into the side his helmet. The other two followed suit as did I. A voice filled my helmet, "Logan!" But I wasn't sure which of the three had spoken. Then the man to my right extended his hand. "Did you hurt your leg?"

For a moment I thought Logan was the name of the man I had replaced, and I wanted to deny it, to say who I really was, but then I realized that the young man was just introducing himself.

They clipped the reflective visor off their helmets, and I understood at once that they had never met before as they were surprised that there was a young woman sitting beside me to my left.

"Joan," she said. "I see that you lost your fly-board? What happened?"

"I fell!" I pointed to my wounded leg, stating my name. "But I got lucky, and only the board is at the bottom of the world right now."

"So cool!" the fourth one said. "I would've liked to be you. I'm Andrzej Jovski!"

Jovski, that was the name written on the side of the helicopter, and the two bodyguards I had seen before were his—I had no reason to be afraid anymore.

Excited from their adventure, they all started talking fast, interrupting one another. I could hear the conversation in my helmet headphones but felt as if I wasn't there.

"I heard a hand came out of the wave," Logan said.

"Yes," Joan confirmed. "A hand with curled up, burned fingers, begging for help!"

"And it had written something down!" Logan added.

"Mene, mene, teke upharsin!" Joan said. "That's what it wrote."

Andrzej Jovski spoke up. "Not just a hand, a whole human!" he said. "They call him The Prophet, and be assured it's not for nothing!"

"Are we going to…" I asked, but stopped just in time, seeing how they all turned towards me. I had wanted to say Atlantic City and might have even asked if a plane would get us over the ocean, to Europe. After all, I had a rich uncle in Paris. But I caught myself, seeing that everything underneath us was pitch black. The helicopter was hovering between light and darkness, day and night, to the west, where the Madness was coming from.

"Yep," Joan said. "We're going back to Wilmington! Such an eerie silence, don't you think so? Nobody's calling because past this *thing* nobody's got any service…"

My God, my heart raced, it was so hard to keep my mouth shut and not give myself away!

Wilmington was still alive!

"Let's hope," I said, "it's only going one way."

"Looks like it," Joan shrugged. "You basically saw for yourself how the *Black Wall* split Salem in two…"

I froze. Salem... Where I'd seen it first, that was indeed where everything had started.

Elise!

Elise was still alive, is still alive. Could it be possible? Everything had begun while I was talking to her on the phone.

Shortly after the helicopter landed at the Wilmington heliport, I started back towards her neighborhood. From the other side this time, straight to the area where I had seen the city divided.

Elise's house was one of the many buildings along that meridian that had been severed into the black. She wasn't at home, but there was a message on her door. Elise was alive. The wall had sliced right through her living room. An unmoving black curtain, several tens of feet high, beyond which my girlfriend was still hoping that her mother was well, in a parallel universe.

I found her a block away at a friend's house just as the note had said she'd be. The next day we moved into a small apartment at the city's western end. I still needed some time to recover.

My uncle in France advised us against selling what was left of Elise's house because it would soon be the most expensive real estate on the planet. The last piece of land, from one pole to the other. He also told us that things were calm in the Old World. They still had three months to live.

"Have fun!" he said at the end.

"What are you doing?" I asked. "Aren't you crossing the ocean? Aren't you coming to the States?"

"What for?" he laughed. "I don't believe in the space program the Americans are talking about. I'd rather open a bottle of champagne on my last night in Paris in three months' time..."

I'll surely suffer PTSD until the time the end does come, but I recovered from the initial shock in about a week. I felt as if I had escaped Hell itself. As nothing vital had been hit, my leg wound was healing well enough for me to be mobile so as soon as we could, we left the apartment and went away from Half-of-Salem for a day.

It was a beautiful spring day. So I took Elise to Washington DC to a café where we had a nice view of the Capital grounds and the hundred famous Japanese cherry trees in blooms.

The air was warm and sweet from the thousands of pink and white blossoms.

"Elise," I said. "Doesn't it seem strange to you that Washington is on this side, not even ninety miles away from the Wall? Don't you feel like the luckiest person in the world, being in the best place on Earth as the end of the world is beginning?"

"You mean because of the beauty of today? Or because all of this will be the last go?"

"Why not both?"

"I do feel lucky, then," she replied serenely. "It's so sad that this happened, yet wonderful in a way that we're forced to appreciate what we have. We need that kind of balance, I guess, even if it will all end in a year and a half."

"It is a balance," I agreed. "You know, I thought initially that this was the fault of some other country, a weapon, but now I realize that Americans are the luckiest of them all."

"The entire Northeast corridor is gone. Philadelphia, New York, Boston, one-in-six Americans dead or displaced, not to mention Montreal and Quebec…"

"Yes, but five out of six Americans still have a home, have this. They didn't go through what the east coast did."

"I don't know what to say, baby. You've been there."

"That's right, you didn't see what I saw," I sighed. "Beyond, people were trampling over one another and fighting for a little bit of space. I saw a man who killed for a bike!"

"The government saved all that they could."

I shrugged, lifted my coffee mug to drink but instead rested it back on the table. "Elise," I said. "How are we going to live in peace, knowing that everything will end in a year and a half?"

She smiled meekly. "Memento mori..." she said. "Anyone's life can end at any time, right? Millions of people would have died in a year and a half anyway. How do you know we won't be among them? That our death weren't already part of some grand design."

"But it's not about percentages or a natural limit right now! We're not talking about old or sick people or accidents... What will parents tell their children?"

Elise dropped her gaze to her coffee and sighed. "I can't answer that," she said. "Mom didn't manage to tell me anything. The Earth, all of this, it will disappear anyway, swallowed by the sun, in about a billion years, maybe another meteor in a million. It's just happening earlier, that's it. Instead of tens of thousands of years, all we'll get are a few moments—making everything that much more special, more intense. Look around."

I did. People at other tables were chatting, smiling, sipping their coffee, as if nothing had happened just a hundred miles away. It was life on the frontline of a war that was getting farther, not closer. For now, anyway, because it was actually coming for us, from the other end of the Earth.

"It's true," Elise went on, "it did catch us by surprise. But that's about to end soon. While the nothingness is crossing the Atlantic, people will know what they have to do. They know now. Europe will not sit idly by. People will migrate east. They will cross the planet to get here."

"And then?" I asked. "When the entire population pack themselves into the last remaining space at the end of the world. What then?"

"Everything will be solved by then. We'll go to the Moon, then maybe Mars. The government's already stated that the entire national budget, all of its resources, have been allocated for this. Russia, China, and India have done the same. We'll make it."

I shook my head skeptically, looking around.

"I don't know what to say, Elise. I can't really believe it. Maybe my uncle was right. Space programs told us of the first colonies being established in a couple of decades—and that didn't include a mass migration."

"They also weren't considering investing more than one-percent of the budget, now they're going to spend it all. But that's not what matters right now," she said. She leaned over the small round table to kiss me.

Right then I felt as if her kiss brought me back to life from a slumbering forest. And then I thought about it. And looked around again, this time with my eyes open.

People were walking around hand-in-hand beneath the blossoms of the cherry trees, not a worry in the world. Poverty didn't matter anymore—nor did riches. No petty ambitions or rivalries. You could see hope for a new beginning in every face.

The Slow Apocalypse had brought death and fear of the inevitable, but it also brought something else, hope and possibility, and maybe, ultimately peace and happiness.

The Dead Lake
Steve Oden

What had been a modern cityscape was now a war-ravaged plain of rubble. Dust devils the size and velocity of small tornadoes sucked ash, grit, and other particulate matter into the atmosphere overhead, where it combined with water droplets to fall as dirty rain. Underground fires burned steadily, sending up flames and a pall of smoke.

At ground level, the blowing ash and smoke often reduced visibility to almost zero. This was when rebel surveillance teams scuttled from holes to reposition their radio interceptors, sensors, and cameras.

The last vestige of the enemy's military had been eliminated in the demolished city. Toy and allied task forces subsequently attacked across the Bloody Bridge to make a lodgment on the other side of the river, from where the final push would begin in a matter of weeks.

Stealthy intelligence-gathering continued, however. The vista from hidden observation posts and remote-control drones was like peeking into the seventh circle of hell. Years of constant battle between the rebellious biomechanical slave-toys and their former masters had left the heart of the city—once a thriving district of sky spires and glass towers—in ruin.

Nothing lived on the blasted ground except rats and roaches. But there was mysterious movement and activity overhead, reason enough for Fuzzy Bear, supreme commander of the Free Toys, to accompany a squad tasked with probing deep into the shell-torn, cratered territory.

His staff adamantly opposed the idea of the sightless battlefield genius risking his life on a mission that could be performed by scout snakes. Their slender rubberized bodies and specialized training allowed them to slither through twisted metal and climb small mountains of debris without detection.

The reptile toys were delighted to have him. This was an opportunity to demonstrate their skill and worth. They did their job so well that many back at headquarters didn't realize critical enemy intelligence originated from the ruins and rubble where cadres of silent serpents kept watch.

"Ssss-ir, beg pardon, but Cap'n Fang report-sss we have three bogie-sss on radar over the Dead Lake. Jusss-t popped up on the sss-creen. No directional vector available. They sss-eem to be hovering," the scout said, raising half her body off the ground and spreading a specialized neck hood equipped with infrared and vibration-sensitive scanners.

Bear hid a grin. He bet she was trying her best to salute. In fact, her black eyes glinted in pride to address the legendary war leader.

"Very well. Your report was informative and timely. Good job! Carry on," he said.

The scout stretched herself even higher, surprised by the unexpected compliment. It was something she'd tell her next clutch of snakelets, if the conflict ever ended.

Bear whispered into the tiny microphone surgically implanted in his paw.

"Sargent Rattler, how long to reach the Dead Lake? I want eyes—er, I mean, a detailed description—of the UFOs showing on radar."

The squad leader promptly replied, "About ten minute-sss, if we take the old sss-ubway tube from the central sss-tation."

The Dead Lake had once been a beautiful greenway in the middle of the city. Fighting had severed the huge supply mains that piped fresh water from the river. The lovely park filled and became a stagnant swamp. When battle raged around it, the water turned red from the bloodshed; thus, it became known as the lake of the dead.

"Gather your squad," ordered Bear. "I want to leave right away."

He added, "And not a word to the command staff. I think you know how they feel about me being here in the first place."

The supreme commander plainly heard a sibilant laugh on the tight-beam radio, but pretended he didn't.

The snakes were quick and silent. Bear wished he could keep up, but he was clearly out of shape. Too much chow and too little exercise. He huffed and puffed, hanging on the snake's tail in front of him and praying the enemy had no super-sensitive sound detectors still operational on this side of the river.

He knew the scout who had reported to him was charged with bodyguard duty. Although he couldn't see with his plastic button eyes, he sensed her: a coiling, writhing blur of motion, checking every pile of debris and yawning shell crater for possible danger.

Sgt. Rattler had already selected a vantage point. A burned-out hovercraft lay on its side, providing an overhang for them to shelter under and raise a periscope. The Fuzzy Bear considered it a miracle that armless, legless snakes used their flexible but muscular bodies to manipulate handling prosthetics.

It took them less than a minute to assemble and deploy the periscope and laser-communication equipment. "Ready when you are, Sss-ir," the sergeant hissed, placing one eye in the ocular to pan the landscape.

"Zooming in on the lake." He tracked upward until a silvery object filled the viewing screen. It looked for all the world like a giant, spinning top.

A torus revolved at high speed around a core, on which was built a hat-like cabin or cockpit. The sergeant could perceive no visible engine, but now he heard a low humming noise.

The flying top held station one thousand feet above the lake, according to the rangefinder. Two similar but smaller tops weaved a defensive pattern around it.

"Are we locked on?" Bear whispered.

"On target and ready," said Sgt. Rattler, nodding to the portable SAM team tracking the large bogie.

If Fuzzy Bear had learned anything while commanding combat toys, it was that you needed to understand your enemy's capabilities before starting a fight. There was no doubt in his mind that the flying tops possessed onboard weaponry. But they wouldn't have drawn attention to themselves—or their amazing technology—if the intent was to attack.

Bear turned to the sergeant with his orders.

"SAM shooters to stand down. Keep recording and transmitting back to headquarters. We need as much data as possible about the UFOs. I also want a tight-beam, coded scramble alert sent to the standby squadron of rocketeers. Urgent order: fly-over at extreme high altitude to conduct sensor scan on flying tops. No aggressive maneuvers. Missiles and guns locked unless UFOs fire first. Repeat the last part of the order to ensure there is no misunderstanding."

Obsidian eyes glittered in the fading light of day. The scout snakes, who'd been primed for a scrap, were confused. They didn't expect an explanation, but he didn't mind sharing his thoughts.

"The UFOs are an unknown. Appearing this close to the time of our final campaign could be good or bad. They probably realize we have the capability to knock them out of the air, yet there they are," he said, ears cocked in the direction of the humming tops.

"I must know why they have shown themselves, what their purpose is. The UFOs represent a new player on the battle board. I won't risk you or our armies until I learn more about them."

Eight scaly heads nodded understanding. Their hoods swelled in pride that their commander would put his fighters first. This was why they followed him, why they loved the old bear. He had once been one of them, a grunt on the front lines, fighting for his teammates. He would never let them down.

Deep in the labyrinthine complex of trenches, bunkers, and pillboxes that represented a last line of defense against the encroaching rebel army, Count Thaddeus convened a meeting of kingdom leaders who still had the grit to fight.

Gone were the pompous youths in their ornate uniforms and the upstart, self-proclaimed barons, princesses, dukes, and duchesses who'd brought this war on themselves through cruelty and stupidity.

The slave toys were living creatures, created to care for the children of parents who abandoned family responsibilities after becoming addicted to new drugs that allegedly opened their minds to other dimensions. Instead of being the next step in evolution of the human brain, the drugs drove the users insane.

The result was mass parental suicides worldwide, leaving only a non-addicted minority of older men and women in charge—and their days were numbered. Confronting the crisis of future generations without family support or oversight, the seniors melded technology, genetics, and bioengineering to produce living toys and robots in which organic brains resided.

Originally conceived as helpers, the toys were trained to raise the orphan children, seeing to their education and life needs until adulthood. A brilliant idea, but one corrupted by the children themselves. Without guidance after the last generation of adults died off, they became slave masters.

Acts of cruelty and persecution devised by the leaders of the child kingdoms became a type of competition: video games made real. Millions of toys died in bloody arenas, on stages, or during horrible experiments meant to create hybrid monsters.

Kingdoms raced to outdo their neighbors. They raised armies and waged wars. Of course, the slave toys were used as cannon fodder, forced to advance across battlefields without weapons or protection. It was slaughter.

Then came the rebellion. Small at first, scattered. Easily extinguished wherever a flame sprang up. The slave toys were persistent and motivated, however. Networks were established, weapons stolen, plans made.

The first major uprising shouldn't have surprised the child kingdoms, but it did. Suddenly, they were forced to confront a large guerilla army. Ambushes evolved into skirmishes, skirmishes into bloody battles, and the battles erupted into war as the toys learned how to fight.

Count Thaddeus had never entertained the possibility that they might lose. But here they were: three remaining kingdoms hanging on by their fingernails.

The young leaders and chiefs of staff did not lounge smugly around the large, polished table. They leaned forward in their seats, all eyes on the small wrinkled man wearing a breathing mask and lab coat.

He was the oldest human any of them had ever seen. By all rights, he should have died and been buried decades ago. Although Dr. Congesto was liver-spotted and hunched, he represented their last hope.

The doctor, a genius geneticist, was rumored to have helped develop the original living toys. Count Thaddeus suspected his price for assisting in destruction of those selfsame creations would indeed be expensive.

The lights in the conference room dimmed. Dr. Congesto started his video presentation. The first image projected on the screen caused several in the room to sit back and chuckle, wondering why the learned scientist would show them a cartoon.

It certainly resembled something on the entertainment nets for younger children: an animated creature, dinosaur-like, that had become a popular video game. A giant predator at least seven stories tall, the monster stomped buildings flat, ravaged the land and ate slave toys.

"Are we going to watch a kiddy show?" asked General Hector, the scornful young dictator of Thaddeus's neighboring kingdom, Ironton. He didn't like the teenager, but conceded that he commanded the largest surviving army after the count's terrible loss at Bloody Bridge.

The doctor's voice was reedy when it came through the speaker in his mask.

"It is good to see someone has a sense of humor in these dire times," he said.

The camera drew back and panned from the floor to the creature's fanged and horn-studded head, then back again.

A figure wearing a hazardous materials suit—Dr. Congesto himself—walked into the foreground of the video. Behind him, a monstrous clawed foot dug deep furrows in steel-reinforced concrete.

"Gentlemen and ladies, may I introduce you to my pet kaiju: Arco Megasaurus," said the diminutive figure.

"Many years in the making, this creation of mine will destroy the rebel toys once and for all. Absolutely nothing can go against this monster. I control it, and my services are available immediately…if we can negotiate acceptable terms."

The room exploded with excited voices. They all wanted to see the kaiju, and a tour of the doctor's underground lab was hastily scheduled. No decision would be made until the new weapon's potential was proven.

"Yes," thought Count Thaddeus. *"This is going to be extremely expensive."*

"Bright Eyes," she said. "My name is Dolly Bright Eyes."

Her piercing blue eyes sparkled like ice. She saluted with her slender fencing foil, then gracefully bowed to the guests—all important rebel army officers—before turning to the shaggy, balloon-headed purple octopus holding a variety of bladed weapons in eight wriggly arms.

Red lips parted her porcelain face in a determined smile. She assumed the *en garde* stance and nodded to her opponent, Captain Sea Foam. In a blur, the combat trainer set himself in motion, a whirling mandala of defense that flashed honed steel edges. There seemed no way for an attacker to get through, let alone resist a countering strike from a heavy sword, cutlass, dagger, battle axe, katana, or glaive.

On her toes like a ballerina, Bright Eyes daintily circled the octopus, staying just out of the longest tentacle's reach. Her prancing steps were like notes of a swelling symphony: each perfectly interwoven with the melodic theme . . . the opening sonata portending a violent clash of silk and steel.

There seemed no way for the gracile fencer to penetrate Sea Foam's tornadic wall of flashing metal. Her light blade, only slightly better than a training prop, would snap in two at first contact with the captain's heavy combat weapons.

Still, she danced, darting back and forth, seeming to probe and pull back at the last millisecond to avoid a slash. Her smile never wavered.

Suddenly, a shimmering, razor-edged fan unfolded in the opposite hand from the one holding her foil. Bright Eye's arm began to weave a pattern above and behind her torso. The fan refracted light like the facets of a gem stone, casting colorful flashes that now counterpointed the lunge and recovery of her thin-bladed weapon.

Still, there was no sound, no clanging of steel on steel. Not yet.

Sea Foam's light-blinded eyes suddenly opened wider. Bright Eyes was standing inside his defense. The sharp point of her foil was aimed at the octopus's mantle, exactly where his central brain was housed.

"*Arett!*" she ordered, her smile becoming grim. The captain dropped his weapons, gladly, and with not a little pride. He was, after all, the combat master, and Bright Eyes was the leader of a company of dolls he had trained to hunt and capture high-value enemy personnel.

Stealthy and deadly, they called themselves the Leaves of Autumn. Their mission was to bring back war criminals for judgment by tribunals of Free Toys and their allies.

Every toy and human in the viewing box stood and began to applaud.

Toy Soldier, all-sector commander for the Free Toy and allied armies, nodded to Bright Eyes.

"*Rassembler!*" she commanded.

From the wings of the training floor quick-marched the four platoons that comprised the Leaves of Autumn. Bright Eyes' three sisters—Dolly Brown Eyes, Green Eyes and Gray Eyes—were her second lieutenants, and led the units.

"Well done, First Lieutenant Bright Eyes," said Toy Soldier. "You, too, Sea Foam, for your work in readying this unique infiltration company tasked with penetrating the enemy's defenses and creating chaos before our all-out assault kicks off."

Turning to those in the viewing box, he said, "It is our hope that the Autumn Leaves can sow confusion and fear among the three kingdoms we now have pinned in place. Their supply lines soon will be cut, and they have no room to maneuver. This does not make them less dangerous. We know that cornered animals fight savagely."

He let this comment sink in for a moment.

"The enemy has bunkered up and, unfortunately for us, seems to be cooperating and sharing intelligence, resources and communications. We number their combined army in the neighborhood of a hundred-thousand fighters, not counting rear-echelon support troops. Many are front-line veterans, eager for revenge."

He heard a voice snarl. "Aye, but many o' the rascals have bite scars on their bums from the dogs on a certain bridge!"

Toy Soldier knew the comment came from the proud Scottish terrier commander, recently promoted Brigadier General "Mac" McCallan, whose toy canines had held at the Bloody Bridge, a costly battle that turned the tide of war.

He waited for the laughter to die down.

"Let me point out, however, the enemy no doubt has nasty surprises awaiting us. Because they are trapped, we must assault over a front that has been sown with mines, ranged by their automatic weapons and artillery, tunneled and trenched, with fortified fallback and rally points and self-supporting lines of fire. There will be bunkers and bastions, aplenty. Expect their armor to be dug in, hull-down, with only turrets exposed."

Unspoken was what everyone expected: close-quarters use of chemical and biologic weapons. The kingdom leaders would sacrifice their own fighters to destroy the former slave toys they hated.

"Finally, our intel indicates the enemy has been working on something big and wicked. A last-gasp, secret weapon of great power. They call it 'Project K,' but we've had no luck in intercepting communications or receiving reports from embedded spies about the nature of this thing."

Toy Soldier added, "This is why we are sending in the Autumn Leaves tomorrow night. The capability of the enemy's secret weapon must be determined and, if possible, thwarted before the attack begins. There is an immediate opportunity: the kingdom leaders intend to gather at a field trial in a few days. Site unknown, but we are working on finding out where and when."

He gestured to Dolly Bright Eyes, who stepped forward and saluted.

"Our mission will be to bag those persons identified as possible war criminals and destroy their vaunted secret weapon—or, at least, disable the thing so it can't be used against our forces!" she declared.

"My warriors are proud to accept this duty. We fully realize our lives are expendable, that there can be no support or rescue. Nor can we slip out. It must be a fighting retreat the entire way because half the company will be disrupting lines of communication and raising holy hell behind the defenses."

She snapped a salute at her commander, to the hurrahs, howls and battle cries of the assembled toy and human leaders.

Toy Soldier returned her salute, proud to command such brave and dedicated fighters, but he also felt the pain of an unhealed wound to his heart. He would carry it until the end of his days. The Princess, his love, was still out there somewhere.

Disfigured and insane, she escaped the Battle of Bloody Bridge, casting off her disguise as the Voodoo Queen before diving into the river. He had hoped to search for her, bring her back to the place she belonged. The continuing war made this impossible. Thus, the fighting must end, no matter the cost.

The freedom fighters were so close now. Their beloved Blind Bear had brought them this far. So much loss of life, grievous injury and physical destruction had been absorbed in order to reach this point. The future would be determined within the week.

Toy Soldier wanted the victory for all those who had sacrificed, but he also prayed the Princess would stay out of the fight, whatever side she took.

He didn't sense her unblinking gaze from the ranks of the Autumn Leaves. The flexible, porcelain-like masks worn by the dollies disguised her scarred features. The freedom fighter formerly known as Princess—and later, the Voodoo Queen—was now a lowly corporal in the Gray Eyes squad.

Toy Soldier was more handsome than ever, she thought. He stood ramrod straight, wide shoulders thrown back at attention, medals glinting on his chest. Too bad she must kill him. First, she must guarantee that neither side would win the forthcoming battle.

Only by ensuring the war continued would her plan to rule toys and humans alike reach fruition. More blood must flow—rivers of it—before her appetite for vengeance was sated.

The Fuzzy Bear and Toy Soldier would be the last to die. It was important, at the moment of their last breath and heartbeat, for them to realize this was punishment for abandoning a loyal soldier and supporter of the cause.

She'd given her all, and they'd taken it and more, leaving an ugly husk in which beauty and love once resided.

They owed her a debt. Payment would be terrible.

"Orders isss orders," said Sgt. Rattler to his frantic squad.

They'd been tasked with protecting the Free Toy supreme commander, laying down their lives for him if necessary. But the blind bear had directed they stay behind while the scout snake designated as his bodyguard took him into the swamp.

The flying top had landed in the lake. It descended to the water's surface, then gently submerged until only the topmost round bulge was visible. Tendrils of steam came up when it touched the water, and a ring of gentle waves lapped outward.

For such a large object, the landing was calm and quiet. Even the humming had ceased. The escort saucers, resembling smaller version of the mother UFO, floated above. Sentinels, apparently.

The bear wanted to get closer, have his bodyguard describe the mysterious thing in the lake. Feel if anything emanated from it on more subtle sensory levels.

"I hate to endanger all of you, just to satisfy my curiosity. We may never get another chance to observe the UFO at close quarters," he said.

"The private there," he pointed to the scout snake who had shepherded him to their observation point near

Dead Lake, "will guide me to a place where we can hide and watch what happens. She will be my eyes and answer my questions. I realize the cameras and sensors have already amassed a great deal of data and transmitted it back to headquarters. Still, I need to get a sense of why it is here and what its purpose might be."

Fuzzy Bear and his guide had slipped away, following a circuitous trail into the thick vegetation of the swamp. Sgt. Rattler followed their progress through the periscope until the figures disappeared in overgrowth. He marveled that their blind leader could move so stealthily.

An hour passed, and the snakes coiled and uncoiled nervously.

The sergeant had decided to send two scouts after them, when the entire lake was suddenly illuminated. A powerful beam of actinic light poured from the UFO's top. An aperture dilated in the side and a walkway thrust outward.

Sgt. Rattler frantically focused the periscope, trying to spot the Free Toy commander and bodyguard. What he witnessed caused his hood to involuntarily spread in alarm.

The harsh light focused on a small silhouette, bear-shaped, followed by a serpentine companion. They were on the walkway, approaching the dark opening. They cast long shadows in the glare, then the next moment they disappeared inside and the aperture snapped shut.

The object hummed, from a bass pitch to a shrill scream that seemed to drill into their skulls. The flying top burst from the water in an explosion of mud and steam, climbing straight up and gaining velocity until it was a pinprick of light lost among the wash of stars in a black velvet heaven. Its escort saucers followed.

Never had the veteran scout sergeant felt so helpless. How was he going to tell the VIPs back at the command center that their military genius had just been kidnapped and taken into outer space by aliens?

The Broken Sleeper

Steven Van Patten

Looking down into his microscope, Dr. Nelson Hayward didn't see anything peculiar in the blood sample. Mild dehydration, perhaps. That would be consistent with what the poor devil had supposedly been through.

"Doctor?"

Nelson turned to see Cynthia, his lab assistant for the past week, standing in the lab doorway. She was especially attractive, but he was resolved not to think about that. He blinked furiously as his eyes adjusted. "Yes?"

"They're bringing in the man that was rescued from the Russians."

He nodded. "Very good. Is he putting up a fight?"

"No," she answered. "Very calm. Why?"

"No reason," he lied.

That is very inconsistent with what I was originally told, he thought as he recalled the report on the subject:

Upon being rescued from a lab Russian scientists hidden in the otherwise defunct Vorkuta gulag, Patient C violently

49

attacked several of the soldiers charged
with his extraction, and succeeded in
killing one by ripping out his femoral
artery. As of the date of this report,
Patient C has hurt seven people in total.
This includes hospital staff. Caution is
strongly advised.

The report was dated a month ago, which made Dr. Nelson all that more suspicious.

"Did the doctor who'd been treating Patient C come with him?" he asked the nurse.

"Yes," she answered as an unsettled look crossed her face.

"Why that look?"

"It's nothing."

"That was not nothing."

She shook her head. "The doctor is... creepy. I can't explain it."

In years prior, he would have felt very comfortable chiding the nurse for being shallow. He might have even hit her with a belittling joke. *We can't all be as attractive as you, nurse.* But these were different times, and these situations required a different attitude. "You won't have to be around the man if you don't want."

"No doctor, its fine. I can do my job," Cynthia said quickly. "But I would probably prefer not to be alone with him."

Nelson nodded absently. "That's fine." He didn't consider himself a good-looking man, and sometimes suspected his wife married him only for his ability to provide a nice house and lifestyle. He was also pretty sure a nurse or two had probably called him creepy during his twenty-three years working at Calfax Labs. A pang of sympathy struck him as he imagined a well-intentioned, socially awkward man of medicine walking into an unfamiliar facility only to be judged by his looks.

A gruff voice spoke from behind her. "Is this Dr. Hayward's office?"

Nurse Cynthia's eyes widened with surprise as she quickly stepped further into the office, clearing the doorway. The visiting physician, dressed in a lab coat like Nelson's seemed to glide out of the darkness out of the hallway as the nurse vacated the space.

The thought that the nurse was being a superficial jerk left his mind the way water evaporates in a small pot. Certain that his initial reaction couldn't have been less welcoming, he quickly tried to recover to a deadpan facial expression. "Oh! You must be Dr. Lemon."

The most alarming thing about the man was his hair, which looked more like metallic strands than anything that should be coming out of a human follicle. Dr. Lemon's nose also seemed to hook, not exactly the way a Halloween witch's might, but definitely malformed. There also seemed to be a glistening under the hooked nose that spread to the man's abnormally thin lips.

Worse still, the man was jaundiced beyond belief, as if the man's liver had died and no one had bothered to tell the rest of his body. "Yes, I am he."

As their conversation began, the nurse's eyes darted back and forth between the two men, as if she were watching a tennis match.

"Dr. Lemon, now that you are here, I have some questions."

"By all means."

"This report you sent seems incomplete, so I was wondering if there was more. Also, I'm a little confused as to why you brought the patient here for an additional blood test you could have administered yourself. That would have saved us the time and energy of transporting your patient, who I am to understand is very dangerous."

Dr. Lemon smiled. "First of all, you said 'a couple of questions.' That was more than more like two questions and a few critiques."

"Say what now?" *He's stalling*, Nelson thought.

Dr. Lemon raised a single hand in mock surrender. "That was a little joke. An icebreaker if you will."

Nelson could feel his cheeks warming. "Charming."

"You're clearly lying about your level of amusement, but nevertheless, I am here to reassure you that the patient is not dangerous. At least, not as long as I am around."

"What are you saying?" Nelson asked. "You've bonded with the patient? To what extent?"

"To the extent that he obeys me completely."

"Sounds a bit 'Frankenstein' to me."

Dr. Lemon frowned. "Nothing of the sort, I can assure you. And if I remember correctly, The Monster didn't obey his creator. He obeyed no one, in fact."

"Apologies. I guess that was my failed attempt at humor. Rife with an inaccuracy, in fact."

"Funnier than mine, accuracy be damned!" Lemon said with a sudden cackle.

Nelson laughed uncomfortably. "I guess we better get to your patient before he starts biting everyone in the building."

Lemon's laughter abruptly ended. "Yes, we probably should."

The nurse watched quietly as the two awkward men exited the lab and turned left towards the main reception area some three-hundred feet down a narrow brick-laid corridor.

Two somber security guards stood waiting in front of the building's main gate, a rotting monstrosity of steel and plexiglass. Between them stood a man who outside of the straitjacket he wore appeared sullen and disheveled. One of the guards held the man's elbow, but he did not seem to notice.

As they drew closer, Nelson and Patient C locked eyes. Nelson gasped. "Jesus...his eyes..."

"Patient C's eyes have been like that since I was brought on to treat him," Lemon explained.

"Is this the result of the experiment?" Nelson suddenly stopped moving forward. It was as if something instinctive told him to not get closer.

"That was my assumption, at first," Dr. Lemon explained. "But then I took the liberty of looking at his social media and I realized that his eyes were like that since birth.

Nelson shook his head. "But they're..."

"Grey," Lemon finished for him when it became clear that Nelson was reluctant to say the word.

"And so much redness surrounding the pupils," Nelson continued. "Like one of those monsters you see on the Science Fiction Channel."

"No need to insult the man."

"You're right," Nelson agreed. "I've been saddled with a lot lately and it's making me tired and cantankerous."

"I understand," Lemon said. "This is a tough business we're in. Administering science and care in an age bereft of logic, compassion, and reason."

"An awful time," Nelson agreed. "I've begun having nightmares about bullies I knew in early school years coming to get me."

"That's terrible," Lemon observed. "But why do you think old schoolyard tormentors would come for you?"

"Because that is what dumb men do. They persecute smart men."

"Nightmares of persecution," a voice said in an almost mocking tone. "Of course, the good news is at least you can sleep."

While the guards stood stoic and silent, the two doctors turned their attention back to the patient they were supposed to be retrieving. He was staring at Dr. Nelson.

"Hmm... he must like you," Lemon observed, betraying some level of surprise. "He normally doesn't speak to anyone but me."

"I'm told I put people at ease," Nelson admitted. "Which comes in handy when you are constantly drawing blood from people."

"I can only imagine," Lemon said before turning to Patient C. "Let's walk, shall we?"

Outside, a thunderstorm broke. Lightning flashed as sheets of rain pelted the building, beating a steady rattling into Calfax Lab's windows. The facility was old, built during a time when construction of such an edifice meant the use of real materials like stone, brick, and mortar. Except for the windows, which would no doubt give way to leaks that would have to be mopped up, anyone inside would be hard pressed to notice harsh weather until they stepped outside.

There was no mention of rain in the weather report, Nelson thought. As a man who had to drive an hour to get to work, he was the sort of fellow that checks weather reports as well as the apps several times a day. He almost said something about it to the four men following him to his office about it, but the words died on his tongue.

Returning to the bloodwork room, he found the nurse prepping for the withdrawal. In his absence, she had scrubbed and put in a hairnet and surgeon's mask. Her energy was different. She moved faster than usual, as if the lab was suddenly the last place in the world she wanted to be.

As Lemon, his two security guards and Patient C filed into the lab behind him, he eased up next to his visibly agitated assistant. "Everything okay?"

She leaned into close to him, causing her scent, an intoxicating perfume, to float into his nostrils. "You left the file open on your desk, so I read it. Why isn't he in restraints?"

Caught off guard, Nelson blurted out the first unfortunate thing that came to mind. "He apparently hasn't hurt anyone in a while."

Over the surgical mask, Cynthia's eyes said what her professionalism would not allow her to verbalize. *Are you fucking serious?* What she did say was, "I'm not doing the extraction. You people don't pay me enough for that."

"I'm sure we don't," Nelson agreed sheepishly.

"Young lady, I can assure you, Patient C is quite safe to be around," Lemon volunteered.

While Nelson marveled at how Lemon was able to hear their whispers from twenty feet away, Cynthia gave a very direct response. "Doctor, respectfully, I was not talking to you."

She turned to give Dr. Lemon a dose of the same indignant glare she'd given Nelson, but ended up locking eyes with Patient C. It was only for a moment, but it was just enough to soften her.

"I understand your misgivings, but I wouldn't harm you, Cynthia," Patient C said calmly. "It's not part of the plan."

Nelson whipped around to face the others. "How the hell does he know her name? And what the hell is he talking about?"

Lemon seemed genuinely flustered. "This is the most he's said since I took over as his caretaker. And as for Cynthia's name, I have no idea what's going on. I can only assume he knows her from somewhere else."

Nelson turned back to the nurse. "Is that true?"

She shook her head. "No, but it's okay. I'll do it. I'm ready."

His eyes squinting with suspicion, Nelson turned back to Lemon. "Okay, let me scrub up, and then we'll do this."

The group silently waited as Nelson walked fifty feet to the sink, washed up and prepped. One of the otherwise emotionless security guards seemed to notice Cynthia's curves as his eyes ran down the length of her frame. Other than that, no one moved or spoke.

Once in his own surgical mask, Nelson rejoined the group. "All right, here we go," he sighed.

With no apparent need for instructions, Patient C slowly made his way to a chair next to where the Cynthia stood. An obvious choice since the chair had an attachment that allowed for the patient to rest their arm while blood was being extracted. As he sat down, he pulled back the left sleeve of the dingy white shirt he'd been wearing. His arm was lean and muscular. He laid it down across the chair's arm extension and looked up with and eerie look of satisfaction on his face.

"One thing still concerns me," Nelson said as he turned back to Lemon. "You previously extracted this man's blood and sent it over last week. As I said in my report, I found nothing out of the ordinary. Why are we doing the test again? And why bring him here this time? Surely, you can extract your own blood samples."

"It has to do with timing," Lemon answered. "I have a theory I am testing."

As Cynthia took up the first syringe in her hand and drew closer to the patient, Nelson raised his hand to halt her. "Hold on, Cynthia. Don't do anything just yet." He turned back to Lemon. "A theory regarding what exactly?"

"That is classified."

"We work for the same organization, Dr. Lemon."

Lemon nodded slowly. "True. But this patient, was rescued by our country's military. There are aspects of his care that fall under a jurisdiction I am not allowed to betray. So yes, I am testing a theory and that theory is classified."

The security guards who up until this moment appeared to be disinterested in anything going on around them suddenly sprung to life. One of them spoke with a pronounced Brooklyn accent. "Is there gonna to be a problem here, Dr. Nelson?"

Nelson looked in each of the security guards faces and watched as the guard who hadn't spoken placed his hand on the butt of his holstered gun. "You guys aren't really Calfax security, are you?"

"We are," Brooklyn answered. "But we are also ex-Marines."

Gun-Butt finally decided to speak. "Semper fi, motherfucker!"

Nelson felt flustered. He hadn't received a physical threat since high school. "Fine, let's get to it then."

Nelson walked towards Cynthis, who handed him a pair of latex gloves. He put them on, never taking his eyes off the seated and quietly waiting Patient C.

"I'm curious," Patient C said. "Does the file explain what the Russians did to me?"

"C!" Lemon shouted. "We are not permitted to discuss that with them."

Patient C's grey eyes found Lemon's. "We are all friends here." Then he turned to Nelson. "To answer your question, Dr. Nelson, your colleague here is intent upon weaponizing me."

"Weaponizing you? How?"

"Stop it!" screamed Lemon suddenly. "Not unless you want to see these two killed!"

"Not these two, no." Patient C corrected. "Maybe *these* two."

As a thunderclap sounded and water from the leaky windows began to fall down the sides of the lab walls, the flash of a lightning strike filled the room. Then, they were all plunged in darkness, everyone suddenly incapable of seeing their own hands in front of their faces. Inexplicable sounds were the only thing available for everyone's struggling senses. A sort of wisping noise as something moved fast through the air around them, almost as if someone were twirling a whip. This was followed by gasps and screams of dying agony that trailed off slowly into silence.

When the backup generator kicked in, partially restoring the lab's luminance, Nelson could see that two tentacle-like protrusions had perforated the chests of the two ex-Marines. The tentacles that held the two men up like rag dolls seemed to be coming from Patient C's midsection. A third tentacle seemed to be wrapped around Dr. Lemon's neck and mouth.

Cynthia screamed and turned away. She covered her mouth to repress her gag reflex as Nelson stood slack-jawed but silent.

"Tell them the truth, Dr. Lemon," Patient C commanded as the tentacle restraining Lemon adjusted just enough to uncover the doctor's mouth.

After a moment, Lemon found his voice. "Yes, it's true, we were weaponizing him. We have been in a race with the Russians to open other dimensions and extract powerful creatures. Some people possess certain recessive genes that make them literal gateways to what some might call hell. But these are just different realms. It's in these realms that elder gods are imprisoned and world-breaker-class-monsters slumber. Creatures who can drive men to madness with a simple gaze. People like Patient C are literal gateways that can be broken if one were to deprive them of sleep for some ungodly amount of time. Many of the subjects go mad, kill everyone around them or even eat their own flesh until they bleed out. But the ones that survive the process become what we call broken gates. Several countries have been looking to harness this power for the sake of dominion over the earth. We need to beat them to it!"

The tentacle adjusted again, muffling Dr. Lemon. "What the doctor had been attempting to do is extract blood from me that could be used to clone one of our more powerful neighbors. His first attempt failed and that is why we are here. As a living gate, I am corporeally here with you, but I am also present in the other dimensions the doctor spoke of. I am also connected to everything that is near me on all sides. This is how I knew your names. If you were to run a DNA test on me now, it would show that I am related to both you, your lab assistant, and everyone else in this room. Of course, that is not true, but that is how the rules of your dimension handle this phenomena. It is a safeguard put in place so that your dimension doesn't rip itself apart."

Dr. Lemon reached up and started pulling at the tentacle restraining him even as the other two protrusions shook the dead ex-Marines off and let them fall to the floor.

"Different dimensions, different rules?' Nelson asked.

"Yes, but just as I currently have your DNA running through me, other creatures draw near. One of them is very close, which is why I was able to grow these tentacles and kill these men before they could bully you into something we would all surely have regretted."

"What about the people you killed prior to that?"

Patient C stood up and rolled his sleeve back down. "That was a creature trying to break through. A cat-like imp that all of humanity would not have been able to stop. It took over my body and would have eventually broken me open and destroyed this world if not for the creature that is currently positioned near me on the other side." His attention seemed to turn back to Dr. Lemon. "And power-hungry idiots like this one would be to blame." With a shake of the tentacle, Dr. Lemon's neck was snapped.

"Good God," Nelson involuntarily shuddered. Behind him, he could sense Cynthia being equally as revolted. "How am I supposed to explain any of this to anyone?"

"You won't have to. However, you may need to clean up."

The tentacles began to retract back towards Patient C's midsection, pulling Brooklyn Accent towards it. Then, like a sort of reverse womb, the midsection expanded causing Patient C's shirt to burst open. A pink-fleshed chasm that could have been a throat without a mouth or a vagina without any sexual or urinary apparatus was revealed. The gaping hole grew wider as the two ex-Marines and eventually Dr. Lemon were pulled in and disappeared. Then, the hole closed leaving only a slit right down Patient C's midsection as his body morphed back to its previous size.

Nelson looked down at the floor, noting the trails of blood and how a mop would, in fact, come in very handy later. "Now what?"

For the first time, Patient C smiled. "The creature that is guarding me on the other side is growing tired. As am I, to tell the truth. Granted, she'll eat those three and be good as new for some time, but neither she nor I can go on much longer like this. You two have to kill me."

"What?" Cynthia shouted.

Nelson finally took a good look at her. She was trembling and clearly terrified. He felt the desire to put an arm around her and comfort her, but even in this situation, he doubted if it was appropriate. "How are we supposed to explain your death? Or the disappearance of Lemon and his two goons?"

"Once you kill me, Algoth will take me, as he took Patient's A and B."

"Algoth?" Cynthia asked. "Who is Algoth?"

"That is her name," Patient C answered. "For reasons I can't fully comprehend, she believes in protecting our dimension."

"How are we supposed to kill you?"

Patient C shrugged. "In this dimension I am just a man. Whatever is easiest for you would suffice."

"Well, you ate the guns along with the Marines, so that's out." Nurse Cynthia observed.

"A bit short-sighted of me, maybe," Patient C said.

Nelson's eyes suddenly shot open from inspiration. "I have blood thinners here. I could overdose you on that. I don't think either of us to ready to do anything more beastly than that."

A faraway look fell across Patient C's face. "You must distance yourself from me now. The drugs may affect you, Algoth."

It took Cynthia and Nelson a second to realize he was not talking to them.

Patient C's eyes closed for a few seconds, then reopened as he made his way back to the chair. "All right, Algoth is gone. But now you must hurry. On the other side I am unprotected now."

Nurse Cynthia's moved with definitive urgency as she prepped the injection. "I really don't want to—"

Nelson cut her off. "I wouldn't dream of making you do this, Cynthia. Besides, we don't pay you enough, remember."

"Damn right," she said.

As Dr. Nelson turned to Patient C and gave the syringe full of Heparin a quick tap with his left middle finger, he looked down to see C's sleeve rolled back up and a vein in the crook of his arm swelling. "I hope this isn't too painful," he said as he finally leaned in. "I'm very sorry this happened to you."

Patient C nodded. "I am too. But there is no other way to resolve this. Plus, truth be told, I really want to just go to sleep."

Nelson nodded. "I understand." As gently as he possibly could, he injected the needle into Patient C.

It felt like an eternity, but they waited silently. As Patient C began to convulse and his nose started to bleed, Nelson grabbed a hand. With tears in her eyes, Cynthia took the other one.

As his mouth filled with blood, Patient C forced himself to say one last thing. "Please don't let this be in vain. Stop them if they try this again."

"Yes!" Cynthia said without hesitation, as Nelson wondered how they would go about stopping two or more governments from doing anything.

"Yes, we will," Nelson finally said.

Patient C closed his eyes for the last time as his body started to melt before them. Cynthia screamed, but not only for the sight. In the other dimension, Algoth had returned to claim the suffering patient. For the briefest moment, all four of them were connected. Dr. Nelson and Cynthia could finally see the great beast protecting the other side from being breeched. It was a squid-like, god-thing floating against a tapestry of stars and purple and red nebulae. The connection revealed that this was a great entity possessed with unfathomable power and knowledge.

In their minds a loud, a powerful voice rumbled. "Let go!"

They did, falling to the floor on their butts in front of the empty, blood-covered chair. Thunder sounded and lightning flashed again as normal power flickered back on in the lab. Then, the storm ended. Except for the puddles of blood, there was no evidence that anything out of the ordinary had happened.

Nelson got back to his feet, then helped his nurse up. "You okay?"

"I saw her," Cynthia admitted.

"Me too."

They hugged briefly then recreated a professional distance. "How do we keep this promise we made?

"I have no idea," he admitted. "But I am going to think about it over a drink."

After a moment, she nodded. "I'll join you, if you don't mind."

"Of course."

Nelson walked to his desk and produced a bottle of whisky from one of the drawers. Without the benefit of rocks glasses, they used a pair of test tubes. He and Cynthia drank silently. It would be at least an hour before they would start cleaning up. Sometime after that they would get their story straight for whoever was going to show up looking for their missing visitors.

Serene in the Light
of the Moon

Daniel Arthur Smith

The heatwave was going into its third week and even in the middle of the night the temperature was unrelenting. Heat radiated from the sidewalks, from the street, from the air itself to smother you, and every indoor space was worse, garages and basements, usually cool in the evening hours, were as hot as a furnace. The five boys wore as little as they could, long thin basketball shorts and sneakers with no socks, tee-shirts loose in their hands or around their neck. Only one of them, Benny, had a shirt on, a dark blue short sleeve collar shirt from Old Navy, but he wore it wide open. They couldn't stand in one place without cooking, without their groins and feet burning with an unseen fire, so they decided the best way—the only way—to cool off was to sneak into the huge community pool over by the school. The lanky teens cut around through the open field behind the school keeping a wide berth of the building so as not to set off any motion sensors they feared may be there. The pool was closer to the street on the other side of the school, but there were houses there and probably motion sensors too, definitely dogs. It was Laroy who was most concerned with the motion sensors. He had been ever since his big brother Jayson was arrested in Buckingham for stealing packages off the porches. They had mad money over there and the packages most always had good stuff, a lot of electronics, but those porches also had motion sensers on their doorbells, with cameras, and when the video was played back there was no denying that Jayson and Jayson's friend Emil were the star of each one. The incident convinced Laroy that the cameras were everywhere and insisted they take the long way around through the field.

The other four boys thought Laroy was extreme, but why take chances? Besides, the field was hot but not as bad as walking down the center of the street. And it was chill too, beautiful even. Beneath the moonlight the world was monochrome. The field, more bronze and brown than green in the day, was a flat sheet of peppered silver, and from a distance, the high chain link fence surrounding the pool was the color of grey stone, and the pool, calm, still.

As they drew closer, the pool compound appeared to grow larger and the fence, taller, so much so that when they finally reached it, the five stopped a few yards short of the chain link and glared up at the top. The height seemed insurmountable.

"What do ya think?" said Chase. "Ten feet?"

"Nah," said Denny. He stepped close to the fence and stretched his hands up over his head to the sky. "I'm six-two and it's twice my height."

"So, twelve then?" said Laroy.

Denny dropped his arms to his side and stepped back. "Fifteen."

Benny dropped his pack from his shoulder. "I'm gonna need to charge up for that," he said, then pulled the cubed bottle of Hennessy from inside the pack, pulled the cork, and took a deep pull. The gulp went down but the gasoline burn caused him to scrunch his face and stick out his tongue. "Ewe," he said. "It's too warm." He shook his jowls to chase away the bitter remanence then held the bottle up to the others. "Anybody else?"

Laroy swatted the bottle away in disgust. "Nah," he said. "That's all you. I don't like brandy."

"It's cognac," said Benny. "Better than brandy."

Jonah swung his arm up and snatched the bottle from Benny's hand. "I'll take it," he said, untwisting the top, then he swilled down a greedy throatful. His reaction was instant. He bucked back half a foot, his arm extending away from him as if the bottle in his hand was to be left behind midair, then he too shook a scrunched foul face. "Woot!" he yelped. "That's nasty."

Laroy shushed him. "Quiet," he said in an exaggerated whisper. "Someone's going to hear us."

"Well," said Jonah. "I hope they bring some chaser because that stuff is nasty going down." He held the bottle up to Denny and Chase as neither had yet to partake but when both declined. "Where's you get this?" he asked as he handed it back to Benny.

"Don't worry about it," said Benny.

Chase offered up the liter bottle of water he'd been carrying. "Here," he said to Jonah. "Rinse your mouth with this…but don't drink it all."

Jonah took the plastic bottle from him and took a mouthful of the water, swished it around, spit it out, then handed the plastic bottle back. "That's warm too," he said.

"It's a hundred degrees in the shade," said Denny. "What choo expect?"

Chase reached out to take the bottle from Jonah, but Benny grabbed it first. "I expect there ain't no shade," he said. "It's damn near midnight." Then he put the bottle to his mouth and tilted it vertical so that bubbles surged up as he took a long drink.

"Hey," said Chase. "Don't drink it all."

The bottle made a popping sound against Benny's lips as he broke the seal away from his mouth. Water trickled down his chin and he wiped it away with the back of his hand. "Sorry," he said. "I was more thirsty than I thought."

"Well, you didn't have to hog it," Chase said, reaching out his hand.

"Taste like warm piss anyway," said Benny.

"So you're thirsty for piss?" said Chase.

"Ha, ha," said Benny. He raised the bottle toward Chase's hand, then, as Chase went to grab it, pulled his arm back and down and alley-ooped the plastic liter bottle up over the fence.

The bottle landed in the pool with a splash.

"Hey!" said Chase. "Watcha do that for?"

"What choo mean?" said Benny. "I was helping you out. Now you don't have to carry it over the fence."

"He's right," said Denny.

"Yeah," Chase said. "I suppose." He looked up at the height of the fence, hooked his fingers in the chain link above his head and with an, "Oomph", jerked himself up. "Time to be Spidey," he said, reaching a hand up higher. Laroy climbed up right behind him, followed by Jonah, who took a running jump. Denny took Jonah's cue, backed away ten feet, then ran and leapt up, grabbing the fence up high with his sneakers a good four feet off the ground.

"Wait for me," Benny said. He stowed the bottle in his pack then struggled to find the zipper. When he finally found it, it got stuck halfway. He pulled and jerked at it, but then seeing Chase already throwing his leg over the top, he pulled the pack's strap onto his shoulder and began to climb. Benny was halfway up when Chase dopped down past him on the other side of the fence, Denny a second later, followed by Jonah. Benny looked up to see Laroy hoisting his leg up and over. Benny swung his arm up for a higher stride to catch up, shifting his half open pack when he did. As he pulled himself upward and heard the hollow thunk beneath him. With his weight hanging from his extended arm, he tilted his head to look down, and sure enough, there on the grass, glistening in the light of the moon, was the cubed glass bottle.

"Damn it," said Benny. He lowered his hands, one at a time to drop himself closer to the ground, then pushed himself away from the fence and landed with a roll. He sat up in time to watch Laroy thud down on the concrete on the other side.

Jonah walked over to the fence to beckon Benny. "C'mon man," he said.

"I need a minute," Benny said, pulling the cork from the liquor bottle. "I used up my gas on the first jump." He held up the bottle. "I need to recharge." Then he took a drink and repeated the process of revulsion, this time his face a little less foul after he shook it.

"Is it any better?" asked Jonah.

Benny nodded. "A bit."

Jonah stepped back from the fence and cupped his hands together. "Throw it over to me."

"No way," said Benny. "It'll smash on the cement."

"I'll catch it."

"Just give me a minute."

Jonah shrugged, spun around, and walked over to join the others. The diving stands stood without boards, a short one and a tall one with a ladder. Denny was standing on the short one, Chase was leaning against the tall one, and Laroy was standing in between. All three were staring down at the calm flat water.

The size of the pool gripped Jonah as he stepped to the edge. "This pool is massive," he said.

"It's long. That's for sure," said Chase.

"Fifty yards," said Denny.

"Meters," said Laroy. He splayed his hands out to outline the pool. "It's eight lanes and fifty meters. It's Olympic size."

"Meters, yards, same thing," said Denny.

"Why is it so cloudy?" asked Jonah.

Laroy pointed upward. "It's just reflecting the sky."

Denny threw his head back. The moon was there, but light pollution from the surrounding neighborhood was too bright for even stars. "There aren't no clouds in the sky," he said. "Just the moon and the black."

"No clouds to our eyes," said Laroy. "But the reflection picks them up. That's refraction."

"That's bullshit," said Jonah. "It's cloudy because it's dirty."

"Nah," said Chase. He bent over the pool, hands on his knees. "It's cloudy because its salt water."

"Whatcha mean salt water?" asked Denny. "Like the ocean."

"Something like that," said Chase. "They use the salt to clean it instead of chlorine."

"I don't know about that," said Laroy. "I was here with my Moms and my little cousins last week, and it was clear as day."

"That's cuz they cycle it at night," said Denny, onboard with Chase's explanation. "That's all. That's how they do it."

"Is that dangerous?" asked Laroy. "The chemicals I mean? I don't want my hair turning no nasty orange color like Shaneal—all patchy and shit."

Chase laughed. "Shaneal's hair is bright as an orange. I don't know what he was trying to do."

Denny kicked off his shoes. "I'm sure it's fine," he said. "It'd smell if the chemicals were too strong." Then he jumped from the pedestal. "Woot!" he yelled and pulled his knees up to his chest to make a cannonball. He hit the water with a big splash that rained down on the deck and sent circles of ripples around him.

"How is it?" asked Laroy, already pulling his shoes off.

Denny shook the water from his face. "It's beautiful," he said, then gave the boys on deck a wide toothy grin.

"Is it cold?" Chase asked, sliding his feet from his sneakers as well.

"No," said Denny. "But it's cooler than the air. It's like bathwater."

Eager to join, Chase and Laroy launched from the deck, each with a big splash and a yelp. Jonah slipped his shoes off too but didn't jump in with them, instead shielding his face from the splashes the two made.

The three in the pool cackled and giggled as they splashed the water with wide flat hands into each other faces. After a round, Chase looked for Jonah, then finding him still up top asked, "What cha waiting for? This is great."

"How deep is it?" asked Jonah.

"I don't know," said Chase. "Deep enough. Jump in."

"It's pretty deep," said Laroy.

"Hold on," said Denny. He extended one hand up high, plugged his nose with the other, and sunk down. Jonah watched Denny's head disappear, then his arm and his wrist, until only Denny's palm and fingers were above the water. Then Denny's wrist, arm, and head appeared again. Denny gave his head a good shake. "I didn't touch bottom," he said. "So, it's *that* deep."

"It's deep enough to dive," said Laroy. He gestured to the tall column behind Jonah. "They bring out boards for events."

Denny craned his neck up over the side of the pool. "I didn't see any diving boards."

"What do ya think those stands are for?" said Laroy. "They mount the boards on the top of those."

"You ever dive off them," asked Denny.

"No," said Laroy. "But I've seen them from the street riding by on my bike." His chin swung over to the garage door on the small cement block building to the side of the pool. "They keep them in there."

Jonah walked behind the short pedestal and started around the corner of the pool. Benny was still sitting outside the fence and noticed Jonah looking over. "Where're you going?"

"I'd rather wade in," said Jonah.

"What?" Laroy said from the pool. "Why don't you just jump in? Don't you know how to swim?"

Chase slapped Laroy's arm then splashed his face. "Cut it," he said.

"What?" said Laroy.

Chase raised his brows. "Let him wade if he wants to," he said.

Laroy slowly picked up the clue. "Oh…" he nodded. "Yeah. I bet the shallow end is nice. Let us know."

Chase splashed him again, joined by Denny. Laroy splashed back and the three began another round.

Jonah continued down the side of the pool. Though the other three boys were still splashing around behind him the shallow end was flat calm, not a ripple. In search of the bottom, he leaned slightly over the edge as he walked but the underwater clouds of the deep end persisted across the pool in one thick hazy underwater mist. When he reached the far corner, he rounded it, then stood with his toes at the edge and looked back. From this end, without his friends close, the pool seemed bigger.

"Huh," he said softly. "Fifty meters." They were indeed far away. Were it not for their voices carrying so loudly in the still of the night they would have seemed even farther. Jonah glanced down at the water again and shrugged. He decided to drop himself in but as he lifted his foot, he swooned, teetered to the side, then caught himself with a quick slide of his foot sideways. The dizziness was accompanied by a tickle in his stomach. Straightening himself, he sucked in a deep breath, let it out slowly, then sucked in another.

The sensations faded. A bit shaken, he ran down the list of what could've just happened. He wondered if something about the haze in the pool had made his head spin and gave him the butterflies. Maybe there were chemicals that didn't have any smell. Maybe it was the heat, that would make sense, or Benny's warm brandy. He never got sick from booze, but it was so hot. Or maybe, maybe it was because he couldn't find the bottom and had no way of knowing whether this end was shallow at all. Jonah wanted heat to be the answer, or even the brandy, but locked in on the last thought as the most likely and looked for some stairs into the pool.

A quick inspection found only the built-in ladders to the side of each corner. A bead of sweat trickled from his forehead into the corner of his eye, producing a sharp sting.

"Okay," he said softly. Then walked over to the side ladder. "It's too hot not too." He reasoned that he could at least lower himself in, and if the pool was too deep, he would simply stick to the ladder and not let go.

Jonah knelt down and swung his foot over and into the water. It was as warm as bathwater, just as Denny had said, but more refreshing than the hot night air. He brought his other foot around, then slowly climbed down the ladder. The water rose to his knees, he expected that, then to his waist, but then it kept rising, past his belly, to the bottom of his chest—the butterflies returned. There was no shallow end. He sucked in a breath, held it, then lowered his foot down to one more rung, and there, it met the flat of the pool floor. Still holding the ladder for fear the ground would drop from beneath him, Jonah let out the breath and planted his second foot down by the first. The waterline was right across his upper chest, his arms, and shoulders above it. He let his fingers rest loose from the ladder and slid a foot back, ready to grab tight again if the pool went deeper from the side. But it didn't. He turned to face his friends, and without lifting his feet, for fear of slipping, he slid one foot in front of the other and made his way toward them.

The haze was to the surface, his body invisible beneath it, he wouldn't be able to tell when the drop off came. So he moved slowly, step by step, toward the center of the pool.

"You coming over here?" asked Laroy.

"Yeah," said Jonah. "Part way anyway."

"That's cool," said Denny. "We'll come over to you."

The three started toward Jonah, then Chase stopped. "Hold on a second," he said. He spun his head side-to-side as he scanned the surface of the water. "Where's my water bottle? It was floating over here a second ago."

Denny shrugged, "It may have sunk."

"I wanted a drink."

Laroy laughed. "Just drink the pool water."

"Ha, ha," said Chase. He pointed to a spot in the water two feet to his side. "It was right here…I'm going to dive down to get it." He sucked in a lungful of air then bent forward and disappeared into the cloudy water.

Denny and Laroy tread the water and waited.

Twenty seconds passed. Then thirty.

"Hey!" Benny yelled from the fence. "Hasn't he been down for a long time?"

Jonah stopped moving forward. "Yeah," he said. "How long's it been? A minute?"

"He's just messing with us," said Laroy. "Probably curled up in a ball trying not to laugh and let out all his air."

"Yeah," said Denny. "A minute's not too long. You can hold your breath for like, I don't know five, ten minutes…"

"You can't hold your breath no ten minutes," said Laroy.

"I can't," said Denny. "But my cousin can."

"Not ten. Maybe five."

"He's on a swim team."

"Well," said Jonah. "That's fine. But Chase ain't on no swim team."

"It's only been a minute," said Laroy. "He'll be up laughing any second. Relax."

"Yeah," said Denny. "Relax."

"Guys," said Benny. "Something's not right."

Benny stood up, approached the fence, hooked his fingers into the chain link, and pressed his face into it. "The water," he said. "The water is bubbling over here."

Denny and Laroy spun their heads back over toward Benny. Sure enough, the water was bubbling in a spot toward the end of the pool.

"Crap!" yelled Denny, splashing into a swim toward the bubbles. Laroy dove into a swim next to him.

"What?" yelled Jonah. "What's happening?"

"It's Chase," said Benny. "He's in trouble."

"Oh no," said Jonah. "No, no, no." He took a step forward, this time raising his foot, then took another.

Denny reached the spot first and dove under, followed by Laroy.

Jonah continued forward, lifting his arms to the side for balance as the water rose to his chin.

The bubbles stopped, the water stilled.

Jonah froze, the water just below his mouth.

"Oh man," said Benny.

"What?" asked Jonah, his head tilted back so he could speak. "What?"

"I don't know," said Benny. "Now they're gone too. The bubbling stopped, and they're gone."

Seconds passed, panic filled both boys as they watched and waited. Benny's chest was about to explode, and Jonah's legs quivered.

Denny erupted from the water, wheezing, and gasping. He kept going upward until his full torso had emerged.

There he stayed. Unnaturally bobbing at his waist. His eyes wide, his face blank, his arms limp as a doll's.

Jonah's eyes spread wide with terror.

"Denny!" screamed Benny. "Denny! What's holding you up?"

The water's surface bubbled again, this time all across the deep end from one side of the pool to the other. Denny pushed up farther out of the water to reveal a long thin black cable, shiny in the moonlight, wrapped around the top of his upper thighs. It was coiled around him, at least three times, and it was constricting, squeezing his legs so tight that with each constriction Denny's open mouth let out a silent scream.

The bubbling surface went black and became a full boil, spouting waves a foot high. Denny bobbed up higher so that only his ankles were below the rapid bubbles revealing the cable to be a tentacle, which curved and arced up beside him. It jerked Denny back down leaving his head and weak arms above the surface then thrust him up again, this time high out of the water above Jonah's head.

Jonah and Benny watched in horror as Denny hung suspended.

The tentacle had the look of wet shiny rubber. It glistened an oily black in the moonlight, its surface scored and scarred, a line of serrated claws along one side, the side coiled around Denny, the tentacle tip wiggling from the coiled section. Darks streaks streamed down Denny's legs beneath where it held tight, dark streaks that were certainly blood.

The boiling water rushed toward the shallow end, washing over Jonah's head, filling his nose and mouth. He spat, sputtered, and mustered strength into his legs to back up, to flee, only to lose his footing in the back pedal and sink backwards. There was Denny above him, then the bright bald moon, then the sting of salt water in his eyes. The warm water rushed around his cheeks and face, into his nose and down his throat. He screamed silent, the salty water filling his mouth. He fought for breath, sucking in the warm liquid, his air rushing out of his mouth and nose in heavy bubbled streams. His ass hit the bottom followed by his back. Beneath the surface it was dark black, Jonah closed his eyes then opened them, no difference. Submerged, he lost all sense of direction. Then his shoulder hit the hard bottom, and in that instant, he regained his orientation. He willed himself to spin, to turn onto his belly. His hands rushed up and planted on the bottom. His chest, his lungs, burned with the salt water. Pedaling his feet, he pushed himself forward and up at an angle. Clawing at the water he made himself stand. His head surfaced and a swoosh of air his ears. He coughed and he barked, but he kept his feet moving toward the ladder. His heart hammered up through his neck, and pounded into his ears—a heavy, loud pounding. He spewed more water from his lungs, saltwater spittle coated his lips and chin. He coughed again, and again, but kept pushing forward. His ears continued to pound, the water continued to boil, but he didn't stop, and he didn't look back.

Jonah reached the ladder, grabbed the highest rung, and pulled himself up. Another stretched reach landed on the deck, and he pulled himself farther, then up and out, to collapse on the deck, where he squirmed his legs onto the deck behind him.

Flat on the deck, he coughed uncontrollably, again and again, his lungs burning fire on each expulsion. When the fit subsided Jonah opened his eyes. They were watery and burning but his vision was clear—and focused on Denny high above the pool in the tentacle's grip.

But Denny was broken.

The tentacle, tightly coiled around his thighs, far below his waist, had shattered his femurs, and as it thrashed him about, it was there at its grip that Denny unnaturally folded and flopped side to side.

"Denny!" screamed Benny. "Denny!"

Jonah heard Benny scream and shifted his gaze over to the fence. Benny was still there at the far-off end of the pool, desperately shaking the chain-link in his clawed hands. Jonah attempted to lift himself from the deck, to get to Benny, but as he rose his stomach cramped, squeezed tight, and he let loose a stomach full saltwater and bile. He held himself on his hands and knees and continued heaving until there was no more to come.

Jonah was left breathing in soft, short, salty breaths. Warm tears ran down his cheeks. His forehead was cool, clammy, his body quivering. His trembling arms threatened to betray his weight. He glanced up again. The water was still a soft boil, but Denny was gone. Benny was silent, his arms hanging limp from the fence. Jonah, ragged and drunk with adrenalin, was dizzy again, but he slowly raised himself from his hands and knees. He moved as if his body was a crude puppet that he could barely control. He was unsteady and nearly fell, but managed to stagger to his feet then, one foot slapping the deck followed by the other, started toward the far fence and Benny. To his side, the sloshing became louder. Jonah looked over to the pool. The water was boiling again. One foot, then another, faster, faster, one foot, then another, a staggered run, a painful hobble. Chest on fire, body on fire, Jonah wanted to cry, to scream. Maybe he was crying, he couldn't tell, everything hurt.

Benny locked eyes with Jonah. His eyes darted to the surface of the water, back to Jonah, to the water. "Faster," he said, too quiet for Jonah to hear. Then louder, "Faster! Faster!"

Jonah fought for every step, thrusting one foot to the front of the other, and with every step he fought his balance.

He'd halved the deck from the far corner. He was almost to Benny.

"Faster!" Benny yelled again, his clawed hands dug into the chain link.

Jonah smiled at Benny. He was almost there.

There was a loud swoosh from the pool. Jonah slowed and half turned his head. Two towering tentacles flailed high above the pool. He froze.

"Run!" yelled Benny.

Jonah faced Benny.

Benny was waving to the side, to the fence a few feet from where Jonah stood. "That way!" yelled Benny. "That way!"

Jonah looked at the fence to his side, then back at the tentacles, wriggling all around the pool. One lashed out and flew toward Jonah. He ducked and it flew past him, over his head. He turned back toward the perimeter fence running along the side of the pool, it was so close. So close. He lunged for it, one foot in front of the other again. Arms stretched out, he reached the fence, clung onto the chain link, and pull himself up to scale it. The muscles of his face contorted from the agony as he pulled himself upward. His arms and legs were weak and sore, but he fought against the pain and climbed.

"That's it," mumbled Benny. "That's it. Over the fence."

The tentacle that had missed Jonah swung back. This time it grabbed him by the midsection and jerked him high up into the air, then down into the deep end of the pool.

It was that fast.

Benny's jaw hung open. Jonah had looked surprised as he was hauled through the air. His eyes were wide, white in the night, his open mouth a dark gaping hole that held no scream.

The second towering tentacle went down after the first.

The boiling stopped. The water stilled.

Benny let his fingers fall away from the chain link and slowly backed away from the fence. He shook his head to shake off the numb sensation that was seizing him, then turned it from side to side in search of his friends, of anyone. His friends were simply gone. The pool calm and empty. It was as it was when they'd arrived.

Benny took another stumbling step back, his heel coming down on something. Benny looked down. It was his cubed bottle of Hennessy. In his state of shock, it was odd, and foreign to him, but he bent over and picked it up. He jerked the cork out with his teeth and spat it out, then put the bottle to his lips. His nostrils flared from the paint lacquer fumes—but he didn't drink. He held the mouth of the bottle to his mouth for a moment, his eyes fixed on the calm water of the pool, in search of a thought that was just out of reach. Then it came to him, and the lost look left his face, replaced by odd contemplation. A realization, a clarity. "Oh, shit," he said. "It's up to me. I have to get help."

He pulled the bottle away from his mouth, looked at in disgust, then threw it to the ground.

Benny turned around to face the school, the field, the moon, quiet still bystanders, then headed back toward the way he and the others had come in to avoid detection. Then another clear thought came. "Wait," he said stopping. He shook his head, to admonish his plan to leave unseen. He wanted attention, all the attention in the world. He wanted all the dogs to bark and the neighbors to yell and the cops to come, and anyone and everyone else who could help. He switched directions toward the gap between the school and the boathouse to the where the houses were closer. He took three steps and heard a loud rush of water behind him. Without stopping he spun his head to face the pool in time to witness dozens of long giant tentacles already reaching up over the fence, flying toward him. Benny threw his arms up to shield himself, but three of the long tentacles effortlessly threw themselves around him—one coiling his upper body, the two others coiling each of his legs. In an instant, he was soaring up, and up, high over the pool. Benny pounded his fists to break free of their hold as the tentacles constricted tight and squeezed the air out of his lungs. He let out a wretched wail which ceased when the top tentacle tore his torso from his waist. His body in two separated halves hung high for a long moment, slowly swaying up against the face of the moon, suspended there by the three faceless tentacles. Then the two coiling his legs ripped them away from each other so that Benny too had become three, and all three descended, back down to the pool, and along the dozens of other writhing limbs, disappeared into the depths with Benny's parts in tow.

The boiling of the water stopped.

The surface softened.

The pool was still.

The night was calm.

Beneath the moonlight the world was monochrome. The field, more bronze and brown than green in the day, was a flat sheet of peppered silver, and from a distance, the high chain link fence surrounding the pool was the color of grey stone, and the pool, calm, still, serene in the light of the moon.

ABOUT THE AUTHORS

Liviu Surugiu is a writer from outside the English-speaking world.

He is editor for the foreign stories in the Romanian magazine *CSF Magazine.*

Among his recent achievements, his prose was selected by The Lunar Codex project in NASA's Artemis program to be taken to the Polaris time capsule that will be buried by the Astrobotic Griffin / VIPER rover on the Moon next year.

On the Earth, his fiction has appeared in *Galaxy's Edge by Mike Resnick (US), Cirsova Magazine (US), Vigyan Katha (India), Galaktika (Hungary), Unfit Magazine (US), Orion's Belt Magazine (US), Gravity City (US), Supersonic (Spain), Nova Sci Fi Magazine (Germany), Teoria Omicron (Ecuador), Maquina Combinatoria (Peru), Algernon Magazine (Estonia), Short Edition (France),* and, of course, in the most important magazines and anthologies in Romania.

He received six Honorable Mention and two Silver HM from *Writers of the Future.* As a Romanian science fiction author, he won forty-one different awards over a thirty years career. Other awards he has received include: Second Place in the *HBO Screenwriter's Contest (2013), Best Novel of the Year 2015, Best Novel of the Year 2016, Best Short Story Collection 2016, Best Short Story of 2017, Best Story 2020, Best Short Story Collection 2022.* He also published eight books in Romania over the past eight years.

Steven Van Patten is from Fort Greene, Brooklyn. After graduating from Long Island University on a full-tuition scholarship, he pursued a career in television production. After paying his dues, Steven went on to stage manage a plethora of TV shows, most recently *The Mel Robbins Show* and *The View*, all the while dreaming up his macabre tales. The storyline of his first novel was born from watching horror movies as a child and noticing a lack of diversity, and character development when people of color were employed. After pouring over historical research night after night, and traveling alone to various locales, including Senegal, West Africa and Osaka, Japan, he wrote the first three installments of the ***Brookwater's Curse*** horror novel series, which featured a 1860s Georgia plantation slave who becomes a vampire.

After receiving much praise, several glowing reviews from various book club heavy hitters, and literary awards for each book, Steven was admitted into the Horror Writer's Association. His next two novels, *'**Killer Genius: She Kills Because She Cares**'* and *'**Killer Genius 2: Attack of The Gym Rats**'*—pitted a hyper-intelligent, socially conscious female serial killer against a well-intentioned African-American detective. It debuted at NYC Comic Con in October of 2015 and was nominated for an *African-American Literary Show Award* for Best Mystery/ Suspense in 2016. Three years later, *'**Hell At The Way Station**'*, Steven's collaboration with Marc Abbott, a horror anthology with a sort of Arabian Knights twist, won Best Anthology and Best In Sci-Free.

Visit Steven at his website brookwaterscurse.com

Steve Oden has worked in the publishing industry–mainly newspapers and magazines–for more than 30 years. Although retired, he provides editorial services on a consulting basis, mainly to corporate clients, and writes on assignment. His newspaper columns have appeared regularly in Tennessee and Alabama publications since 1980, winning awards from the Alabama Press Association, University of Tennessee-Tennessee Press Association, Society of Professional Journalists, National Rural Electric Cooperative Association and several wildlife conservation organizations.

Daniel Arthur Smith is a USA Today bestselling author. His titles include *Spectral Shift, Hugh Howey Lives, The Cathari Treasure, The Somali Deception*, and a few other novels and short stories. He also curates the phenomenal short fiction series *Tales from the Canyons of the Damned* and *Frontiers of Speculative Fiction*.

He was raised in Michigan and graduated from Western Michigan University where he studied philosophy, with focus on cognitive science, meta-physics, and comparative religion. He began his career as a bartender, barista, poetry house proprietor, teacher, and then became a technologist and futurist for the Fortune 100 across the Americas and Europe.

Daniel has traveled to over 300 cities in 22 countries, residing in Los Angeles, Kalamazoo, Prague, Crete, and now writes in Manhattan where he lives with his wife and young sons.

For news and updates visit danielarthursmith.com